A Heart Surrendered

Joy K. Massenburge

HARAMBEEPRESS

A HEART SURRENDERED BY JOY K. MASSENBURGE
Published by Harambee Press
an imprint of Lighthouse Publishing of the Carolinas
2333 Barton Oaks Dr., Raleigh, NC 27614

ISBN: 978-1-64526-184-1
Copyright © 2019 by Joy K. Massenburge
Cover design by Elaina Lee
Interior design by AtriTex Technologies P Ltd

Available in print from your local bookstore, online, or from the publisher at: ShopLPC.com

For more information on this book and the author, visit: www.joykmassenburge.com

Brought to you by the creative team at Lighthouse Publishing of the Carolinas (LPCBooks.com): Eddie Jones, Edwina Perkins, Kay Coulter, Judah Raine, and Lucie Winborne

Library of Congress Cataloging-in-Publication Data
Massenburge, Joy K.
A Heart Surrendered / Joy K. Massenburge 1st ed.

Printed in the United States of America

PRAISE FOR *A HEART SURRENDERED*

Joy K. Massenburge tells a story with heart, compassion and wisdom. I cared so much about Sharonda, even now my heart melts for all she went through, trying to be faithful and find her own happiness while pressured to do what others saw as her duty. All the characters with their complexities came fully to life through the music, their ministries, their strengths, weaknesses and struggles … and their love. Ah, I am still smiling.

~Mary Connealy
Bestselling author
Aiming for Love (Brides of Hope Mountain series)

Joy K. Massenburge brings a fresh new voice to Christian fiction. I love this book. The romantic tension in the story is wonderful. Joy doesn't skirt around difficult issues. Her characters grabbed my heart and didn't let go until I read the last word.

~Lena Nelson Dooley
Multi-published author, speaker, and mentor

A Heart Surrendered is a sweet, southern romance that packs a message for everyone who has ever struggled between doing what's expected of them or following the heart. Joy's writing will mosey into the scenes. Enjoy the journey with the characters and find many, many laughs along the way.

~Michelle Stimpson
Bestselling Author
Mama B Series

A Heart Surrendered is a hilarious yet touching romance about second chances. Massenburge weaves rich characterization with a minefield of family interference to concoct this delectable novel.

Acknowledgments

I must thank my husband and kids for supporting my dream to write fiction. Too many times I've worked through the night, failed to cook, and totally ignored cleaning chores. There is the Lena Nelson Dooley Critique group and my online critique partners. You know who you are. Thank you. No book is written alone. A special thanks to my editor on this project, Edwina Perkins and to my launch team, words will never express my gratitude. Thanks for spreading the word. Finally, I say thanks to the award-winning authors who took the time to endorse this work.

DEDICATION

This book is dedicated with love to my spiritual covering, my First Lady Dr. Cynthia Morrow who encourages me to walk in the calling on my life.

Chapter One

Sharonda pulled the lapels of her pink blazer together with trembling hands. Despite several attempts, the third button never slipped into the hole. Even if it had, she wouldn't be able to lift her arms. The tightness pinched across her ample bosom.

"I hate Sundays," she said through gritted teeth.

A door slammed from the hallway. Her mother's shouts from her parents' bedroom stopped. Dad had taken a verbal beating. He might be esteemed as the great Pastor Broddrick Peterson at the church, but in this house, until he was elevated to Bishop, First Lady Marianne would find something to nag about.

Sharonda sucked in her breath and tried again to fasten the resilient button. She exhaled in defeat. The jacket remained open and exposed the matching camisole beneath.

Rather than rehang the two suits she'd tried on, Sharonda scooped them from her closet floor and stashed the garments in the back corner. After service, she'd fill a thrift store bag with everything too snug. That meant half of her wardrobe.

She eyed the hat box stored high on the shelf. Another something pink. Paste a label across her chest and she'd pass for a human billboard for Pepto Bismol. "Not today." She grabbed her Sunday curriculum satchel and purse from the hook instead. Crossing her bedroom to the bureau, she placed her hand on her Bible and traced the lettering.

Mother won't approve. Get the hat.

If Sharonda showed up at the car without her hat, Marianne Peterson would subject her to a tongue-lashing far worse than Dad had received earlier. Sharonda placed the Good Book in the crook of her arm and walked back to the closet. Dread weighed so heavily, her shoulders slouched with each step. Although a small thing, she would yield to reclaim a semblance of peace—something this family no longer shared.

Stretched, she nudged the corner of the hat box with her fingernail but only managed to scoot it further back. Again, she stretched. A pain ripped through her abdomen. Sharonda clenched her jaw against the scream straining to erupt. After the cramp subsided, she leaped. Her nail nipped the bottom and knocked the cardboard prison down from its lofty perch.

The box smacked her in the face. The wide-brimmed, sequined headdress and the newspaper stuffing dumped at her feet along with the Bible. Swallowing hard, she pressed a hand to her left cheek and clutched her stomach with the other. Please, not now. She ticked the weeks off on her fingers. Only three had passed. No time to check if her cycle had hit or change clothes. Sharonda turned at the movement coming from the opposite side of the room.

Her twenty-five-year-old sister, Janice, flopped onto her back and yawned from her bed. No telling what time she'd slipped into the house after a night of partying. She shook her head. Why did she still share a room with her sister? Approaching thirty, Sharonda *should* have her own place.

"Bag Lady, why scurry around so? Mom's loud bellyaching got you doubting yourself this morning? Don't worry, one look at you in that get-up and the saints will know you're a good pastor's daughter," Janice said.

Sharonda pulled at the hem of her jacket. "Shut up and get your lazy behind out of bed. Time *you* attend service for a change."

Propped on one arm, Janice frowned. "Nope. My make-believe days are over. You ought to join *me* and stay home. It's liberating."

2

"If emancipation is your goal, why are you still living here?" Sharonda snagged the scrunched newspapers, re-stuffed the hat's collapsed dome, and then crammed it back inside the box.

"It won't be much longer, then I'm out of here. What's your excuse?"

Sharonda crossed her arms. "It's best I live here." She looked toward the prescription bottles on her dresser. "Mother worries about me. I can't add to the stress in her life."

"Worries about you? Or what she'll have to do if you're not here to answer to her every whim." Janice snorted. "Lost. I can see it now. Once you marry, she'll have you and your husband moved up in here." She ran a hand over the pink wallpaper. "If you ask nicely, maybe Mom will let you redecorate."

Everything matched—twin sleigh beds, comforters, lamps. Even the black ballerina wall décor to accent Janice's dance recital pictures. Had Mother ever stopped to consider what someone else wanted? The room would be yellow, bathed in the warm beauty of sunflowers if she had. An accent to the honor cords on display in Sharonda's graduation shadow box.

"Dad is a candidate for the Suffragan Bishop vacancy. His chance can be ruined because of you and that selfish brother of ours." Along with the hat, Sharonda retrieved her Bible and walked toward her side of the room.

"That's stupid. Travis is a grown man. And *I'm* a grown woman. If the organization holds Daddy responsible for that, they don't deserve his servitude."

Balancing the large box, Sharonda dropped the container on top of her eyelet comforter along with the purse and satchel. She'd have to reorganize if she was going to get her stuff to the car in one trip.

Janice kicked her long legs free of the encumbering sheets as she sat up, stretching tall and lazily. Give her a scratching post for her unsheathed claws and she'd have the makings of a Persian feline.

The muscles in Sharonda's shoulders bunched into a knot. Dull pains radiated up her neck. "It's our convention. At least come to the second service."

3

"No." Janice yawned.

"If not for our parents, then the family. Mother's showing signs of another mental break. Like it or not, she is the glue. Think about somebody besides yourself."

"God's in control. Ain't that what you church people say?" She swung her legs over the side of the bed and wiggled her toes into cashmere slippers. "I'm finding my own way. Jesus already gave his life, so the church doesn't need mine." She shook her long, wavy curls. "The Holy Roller lifestyle ain't worth the sacrifices. And I'm not talking about those black sponge rollers you torture your scalp with." Janice laced her fingers and stretched her arms overhead before relaxing them at her side. "Seems to me you've allowed that legalistic church to convict you to give up Mr. Wonderful. And don't pretend he doesn't exist."

Warmth rushed through Sharonda's core at the mention of Carl Ray.

"You gave up that fine man for what? This?" Janice fanned her hands toward Sharonda, from head to toe. She scoffed then hugged her pillow to her chest.

The grandfather clock in the living room chimed.

"I've got to go." Sharonda strapped her Sunday school bag across one shoulder and the matching pink purse over the other. She gripped the hat box's corded handle, tucked her Bible under her arm, dropped her chin, and headed for the door.

"What you running from? Don't give me a hard time about church attendance until you can look at me—without a sign of that old guilt—when I make mention of Carl."

Sharonda halted as she gripped the brass handle. The coolness extinguished the fiery retort at the tip of her tongue. She turned to face her sister. "I don't know what you're talking about," she stammered, lifting her head.

Janice flung her pillow aside and approached.

Bed head shouldn't look as good as it did on her beautiful little sister. Her silk chocolate nightie settled mid-thigh and accentuated lean curves and shapely legs.

"Stop it." Janice put her hands on her hips.

"I didn't do anything."

"You were sizing me up. Comparing. Tell me it ain't so." Janice hiked her brow.

Sharonda blinked. Renewed images of her sister's perfect body silenced any rebuttal.

"Stop being Mom, comparing everything and everybody. How you let that woman convince you Carl Ray's fame changed how he felt about you is beyond me. He always wanted you for *you*." Janice tapped Sharonda beneath her chin. "Tell the truth. You love him. Why this sham of a marriage to Pastor Brice? You're going to ruin your life to please Mom?"

"What Carl Ray and I shared … It's been over." Sharonda looked down. "Juvenile affection at the most."

"Liar."

"Brice agrees to start a family right away." Sharonda pulled her purse strap higher on her shoulder.

"He's too old for you."

"Seventeen years on a fit man is not that big of a deal. Not to me anyway." Her stomach, riddled with fibroid tumors and endometriosis, constricted. Sharonda pushed a fist into her side. "I've got to go. Can't make Dad late."

Janice thumped the box. "Your big hats, doctorate in theology, and frumpy clothes don't fool me. The outer appearance may look like the missionaries on the front row, but my big sister is somewhere under those layers you're packing on. When you come to terms with the Sharonda who's human, you'll be able to look me in the eye and tell the truth."

"You're so … full of yourself." Sharonda blinked away the tears stinging the corners of her eyes.

"Stop pretending to be someone you're not."

Sharonda glared. "Until you experience the pain I suffer, don't you dare preach at me."

Janice wagged her manicured finger. "No matter how many church services you attend, we both have a reservation for the lake of fire. Liars and revelers." Janice cackled. "This party girl is having fun getting there. What do you stand to gain for your piety? A lifetime serving Mom and Dad? Marriage to a man who loves the thought of being the next pastor of New Hope more than desiring you? That would be a waste, sis. Now look me in the eye and tell me you don't have feelings for Carl Ray." Janice cupped the side of Sharonda's face.

Her heart skipped at the mention of Carl Ray. Sharonda's gaze climbed a path along Janice's long neck to her dimpled chin. She took in her sister's full lips. Her gaze stopped at the bridge of Janice's pert nose.

"Told you." Janice snorted. "You're no better than me." She turned, swishing her hips from side to side as she returned to her bed. She shook the sheets, then crawled between them with her back to Sharonda. She had the audacity to hum.

Sharonda tried to drown out the lonesome lyrics. What's love got to do with *anything*? She fled from the room, stopping outside the door.

Janice yelled, "So what if you turn thirty in three days? Have the hysterectomy and adopt. But if you close the door to a future with Carl, don't be mad if I open it."

Her sister's mocking laughter riled her. Sharp pangs shot through the very womb that threatened to steal Sharonda's hopes to ever carry a child.

She stepped down the hall and through the modest house to the sound of a honking horn.

"I'm coming." She paused, placed the hat box on the hall table, then charged out of the house.

Mother's stately profile, decorated in a single plumed hat, filled the passenger side. The driver's seat of her parents' Mercedes remained empty.

She sighed with relief that she'd beat Dad to the car. She slowed her pace, heated from the extra exertion in her three-piece suit. She worked to get all her bags to one side. Stuffing the Bible in with the curriculum, Sharonda peeled her jacket away from damp skin. Moving everything to the opposite side, she freed herself and folded the blazer over her forearm. Sharonda climbed into the back seat, behind her mother, and closed the door harder than necessary.

"Sorry." Not really. She flung her jacket across the leather upholstery and tugged at the waistband of the Spanx rising up over her stomach rolls as she fought to breathe.

Mother turned in her seat. "I thought we agreed you'd wear blue. Pink is a poor accent to my magenta."

Sharonda pulled at the hem of her camisole. "Wardrobe malfunction."

"And where is your hat?" Mother lifted her too-perfect nose, everything about *her* petite and sassy while Sharonda took after the Peterson women—big-boned and reticent. "Not that I miss seeing the box strapped to your arm." She used her First Lady of New Hope Church voice. Opening her compact, Mother faced forward and dusted Rich Bronze powder on her smooth skin. She followed up with a precise dab of gloss to her lips.

Mother accomplished her natural beauty appearance with help from the MAC cosmetic counter. Illusions of perfection were her masterpiece. Sharonda had been her reluctant apprentice for years.

She crossed her arms. "My hands were full."

Mother capped the gloss and flung the container in her purse before she reached out, tilted the rearview mirror, and stared. "If you got in a habit of wearing the hat instead of carrying it around like a piece of luggage ..." She popped her shiny lips. "Problem eliminated."

"But my head hurts when I wear it all day." Sharonda sounded like the sixteen-year-old who had gained another ten pounds and lost her mother's approval. "And besides, I don't have a safe place to store the hat when I pull it off."

Mother gave a dismissive wave over her shoulder. "Hurry. Run in the house and get your head covering before you make us late. Silver. Gold. Something to offset all that pink."

Sharonda wrung her hands in her lap. "Can't I just go without it this time?"

"Where did I go wrong in my parenting? You know what is expected of the first family." Mother threw her hands up. "And it's convention time. The elders require a woman's head to be covered. Of my three children, I wouldn't think I'd have to explain to *you* the importance of setting a good example. First your sister left the church. Then your brother moved out. What are we supposed to do without a minister of music? We'll lose the band. Our congregation will split."

Sharonda exited the car to escape her mother's rantings—an event occurring way too often these days. Being the preacher's kid came with too many demands.

She trudged back toward the house. Pushing through the door, she banged her arms still laden with the purse and Sunday school satchel she should have left in the car. How had her organized day turned into such a tangled mess?

"Aren't you headed in the wrong direction?" Dad passed her on his way out.

"Sorry, I have to grab my *pink* hat." At the decorative hall table, she yanked the box's cord on her arm, disturbing the ceramic angels. She reached out to realign them and stopped. Forget it. She spun around and hurried out. Once in the car, she clicked her seatbelt as they backed out of the driveway to maneuver through the sleepy neighborhood. Her parents' idea of being late would put them at the sanctuary over two hours before the first service.

Minutes into the half-hour commute, her mother twisted around to face her. "Why are you so quiet? Are you ill?"

"Enjoying the scenery, Mother." She bit her lip and adjusted her skirt, not sure if the discomfort at her waistline was emotional or a flash-flood warning. She ran a hand over her abdomen. No time to be bedridden today.

Her mother faced forward. "Good. There's too much on the schedule for me to handle by myself. I don't know what I'd do without you." Mother's praise fell flat on Sharonda's tired ears.

Tired of being Mother's go-to person. Tired of her own needs being overlooked.

Tired of being.

They passed the Jefferson spread. Sharonda loved how the big house and barn were set in the middle of rolling green hills. On so many acres, the Longhorns seemed to be roaming free.

She envied them.

Too soon, Dad parked in his designated spot to the right side of the church.

Sharonda lagged behind her parents' entrance into the vestibule and down the hallway that led to the administration offices.

A melodious rhythm rose from the music room, a familiar voice accompanying the key's major chords.

Startled, she tripped.

Her satchel fell from her shoulder and clattered against the tiles, dumping her Bible for the second time. Strewn at her feet were her study notes, jacket, and Sunday school workbooks. She laid a hand over her chest to calm her racing heart.

Mother turned and rushed to her. "Baby?" She yanked the lace-trimmed hankie from her purse and blotted Sharonda's forehead. "Broddrick, it's happening." She turned a worried expression toward her husband. "Look at her. She's clammy. Sweat's beading her top lip, and her arms are full of goosebumps."

Sharonda ducked out of reach. "Mother."

The music from the praise team practice room—which caused her violent reaction—faded.

"I'm good. Probably too many layers. I'm wearing the new girdle you suggested." She mentioned the garment to distract her mother's busy hands.

Dad cleared his throat, then walked down the hall. Any mention of what he'd refer to as mother-daughter stuff was his signal to escape.

"Go adjust yourself, then." Mother tucked a soft curl beneath her hat as if one had dared to stray under her watchful care. Unlike Sharonda's thick flat-ironed hair that she still struggled to tame. "However, if it's your menstrual, you and Brice best consider an earlier wedding date. It hasn't been a full three weeks since your last episode." She trailed the path toward Dad's office.

"Hmph." Mother better be glad she still agreed to marry the missing-in-action preacher. No need in rushing into a life of misery. But then, wasn't he her only chance at having a baby? She stamped her foot, sending the papers at her feet in all directions. Who had taken her brother's position as minister of music?

She hiked her skirt and strong-armed the tight Spanx. The elastic at her stomach lowered enough for her to bend and collect the scattered curriculum.

"Let me help you."

Her head lifted in the direction of the intrusive bass. That voice belonged only to one man—a sculpted work of art—and the owner of the melodious sound that had come from the music room.

Carl. Ray. Everhart.

He knelt beside her and shoved the last book into her bag. Offering a warm smile, he stood before she could react and helped her up.

Sharonda stared into eyes that reminded her of glowing embers in a fireplace on a cold winter night.

Carl Ray hugged her. "It's so good to see you. How are you, Sharonda?"

She wrapped her arms around his narrow waist. A cloud of the sweetest spices washed over her senses—deep, sensual, and earthy. If she didn't know better, she'd say he'd taken a puff from a tobacco-filled pipe.

"Let me look at you." He stepped back.

Sharonda snatched her tote from his arm and held it against her front. For what? Cover? She'd need every bag they sold at Walmart to hide the pounds she'd packed on. If only she could disappear.

He tilted his head sideways and scrunched his brow. "How have you been? I left you messages, but you didn't return my calls."

She clutched the bag tighter. Words crashed against her skull, trapped as if someone had stitched her mouth shut.

"We need to talk." He reached out as if to stroke her cheek.

I'm sorry I lost control. His message resurfaced. *It never should have happened.*

10

Sharonda stepped back, shaking her head. "No need." She took a deep breath, exhaled, and then pressed her lips together. Once, she'd been Carl Everhart's girl.

He closed the distance between them. "I really should—"

She held up a hand. "Apologize? I've given God everything else. I can have one night."

Sharonda backed away and tried to steady herself.

He rested his hands on her shoulder. "What happened was wro—"

"Beautiful." She turned and ran. No one, not even Carl Ray, had a right to tamper with her memories.

Chapter Two

Carl leaned against the door to the music room. He turned his head toward his shoulder and sniffed. Sharonda's alluring aroma clung to the fibers—black raspberries drizzled in warm vanilla cream.

His thoughts lingered on their shared embrace. His arms remembered her healthy curves. Soft thickness—pressed down, shaken together, and overflowing—an abundant blessing. His core warmed, stoking coals best left cold.

Renew a friendship. Nothing else.

Carl reached under his button-down shirt and ran a hand over the puckered scar along the right side of his stomach. Women. Money. Fame. All vanity. Had any of it mattered when he faced death on the operating table?

He lifted his eyes to the corkboard ceiling tiles and mouthed *Thank you.* A lump grew in his throat. Carl shook his head.

The scent of sweetened berries flooded the air around him. "Have mercy, Lord." He removed his outer shirt, wadded the crisp material into a ball, and stuffed it into his duffel.

He slid onto the piano bench.

How could he respect Sharonda's obvious desire to be left alone and do what God called him to do? Carl banged his fists onto the black and whites.

"That bad, huh?" Derrick—his childhood friend—crossed in front of the piano. Drumsticks protruded from his back pocket. "I warned the guys not to get used to you being here."

"You know me better than that. When I give a commitment, I stand by it."

Derrick laughed. "Uh-oh, I hit a nerve. Ever think to take some of that money you made on the road and see a therapist?" He sat behind the drum practice pad. "T-shirt? You wearing that for Sunday morning service? Bad business. With the church *and* the band."

Carl banged the keys again.

"Don't think that'll work for praise and worship." Derrick tapped the pad, then twirled his right stick. "Is Sharonda still not talking to you?"

"Maybe *you* should do *less* talking and more playing." Carl fingered the strains of an old hymn. "Better?" He wanted to open in faith—proclaiming it is well with *his* soul—leaving personal issues in their rightful place.

His friend laughed.

Carl rested his hands in his lap. "Your boys are late. Everyone reports here at eight on Sundays."

"You need to chill. Church doesn't start until ten." Derrick adjusted his cymbals.

"Getting here a few minutes before doesn't allow us to prepare our minds—or our hearts—for worship. It takes the Word of God resonating in our spirit to minister to the people."

"Minister?" Derrick frowned. "New captain wants to rock the boat, I see."

"No, but I do want to be about my Father's business."

"Who talks like that? I understand you had a life-changing experience, but you're doing too much. Too soon. Slow your row. You'll wreck this ship before you can get it into water."

Carl shook his head. "Tomorrow's not promised. I have to do what I can today."

"Did they operate on your tongue on that table? You look like Carl, but you sound nothing like him." Derrick twirled his left drumstick.

Carl thumbed through his sheet music. "This is the new me. As soon as everyone arrives, I'll give the run-down on my expectations."

"Advice is free. Need a Personal Relations Specialist? That'll be fifty dollars."

This time, Carl laughed.

Aaron entered, his hands weighed down with an amp and bass guitar. Grey hairs highlighted the close-cut sideburns of the older man whose athletic build gave him the appearance of someone younger. His case slammed into a metal chair and sent it tumbling. In his attempt to upright the chair, he bumped his stand. Sheet music dumped on the floor.

Carl approached. "Let me help you." He positioned the amplifier while Aaron unpacked the guitar.

The older man gave a curt nod. "Thanks, boss." A thick gold chain dangled between the V-opening of his fitted dress shirt.

"We're a team. Call me Carl." He extended a hand.

Aaron raised his chin. "Is that what you're wearing?"

Carl rubbed his rejected hand down his pant leg. "No."

One by one, the three remaining stragglers ventured into the practice room and readied their instruments. All gave him the same look of disapproval. He doubted all of the contempt dealt with his wardrobe.

Carl sighed. What would he have to do to earn their respect? He headed for the coatrack in the back of the room and pulled a new shirt and jacked off the hanger. Days on the road taught him to keep a spare.

Back at the keyboard, he lifted a red folder. "Please review the music packets I placed on your stands. Some of the material you've played in the past, along with three songs I've written and recorded."

Everyone but Aaron opened their folders.

"That's what's up." Paul saluted as he pulled the guitar strap over his dreadlocked man bun. "I always wanted to write my own songs. Maybe you can give me some advice."

"Sure." Carl smiled. Win one at a time. "Guys, please be familiar with every selection by the time we meet for practice Friday with the vocalists."

"Why two practices?" Aaron stopped tuning his bass. "When Travis was here, the vocalists joined our practice after Thursday night Bible Study."

15

Carl held the musician's gaze. "To efficiently work with singing parts in addition to the instrumentals, we need more than an hour-rehearsal. Unless you want to extend our current practice sessions."

The men grumbled.

"What we have now will not work. Changes are coming." Carl returned the folder to the piano and nodded toward Derrick. "Our reliable drummer will make sure everyone is aware of dates and times. You're expected to be prompt."

Aaron rifled through his folder.

The others focused on Carl. He continued, "Sunday school class will be here in the practice room. The more we know God's Word, the closer we are to Him and the better we're able to hear the Spirit direct us in praise and worship."

"Are you saying Sunday school is now mandatory?" Paul unbound and tossed his long locks. A burst of scent similar to corn chips marinated in sauerkraut permeated the small space around the musician.

Carl studied the young musician. His starched jeans and dress shirt appeared clean. They'd judged him by his looks alone. Should he address hygiene? "Consider it a necessary requirement to fulfill our jobs effectively. A judge enters the courtroom wearing his robe, prepared to walk in the authority the law gives him."

"This ain't a court of law." Gerald's short pudgy hands danced over the bongos. The percussionist's bald head—oiled to a sheen and resembling a black bowling ball—remained down.

Carl tugged the cuff of his sleeve in place. "You're right. But, if you're not prepared spiritually, the church has failed. I'd rather see you in the general audience, worshiping with like believers and getting what you need instead of hiding behind your talents, thinking that's enough."

"Amen." Derrick said it in a way that steered Carl toward safer waters.

He sat at the piano. "Shall we proceed?"

Derrick nodded.

A harmony settled around Carl as everyone joined in. Nothing bonded musicians together like creating music.

~

Sharonda survived the first service, then hurried into the ladies' room near the foyer. Her stomach muscles spasmed, evidence she'd waited too long. First Lady Marianne Peterson trained her girls well in the art of church etiquette. If she dared walk the aisle during church for a bathroom visit, she'd earn Mother's scorn. Sharonda rushed inside the first of three stalls. No time to layer the toilet seat with tissue on both sides, front and back.

Sharonda tapped the handle of the toilet and huffed as she worked to get her clothing in place. Why didn't the air conditioning blow heaviest in the bathrooms? If builders ever tugged pantyhose over moist skin, they'd have insisted on a cooler environment.

She inched the nylons up over her knees, shimmied, hopped, and tugged until the inseam stopped mid-thigh. She inhaled and blew, sounding like a whale surfacing, and tugged some more. The next sound caused her to collapse onto the toilet seat. *Really?* She pulled off the ripped pantyhose. Grrr.

The bathroom door banged against the stop.

Sharonda stilled.

Laughter preceded stilettos clicking against the tiled floor. The ladies conversed at the large basin vanity positioned against the wall outside her stall.

"I can't wait for second service to begin. Did you hear?"

"*The* Carl Everhart, from the gospel stage play, *You Are Your Brother's Keeper*, is leading praise and worship."

Squeals erupted.

Sharonda covered her ears until they calmed. Did anyone use the facilities anymore for the original purpose?

"Makes me want to praise God as well as some other *thangs*. Don't look at me like that. You know that man's voice is sexy, and he's so good-looking. A light-skinned brother, tall, and great hair. Those deep waves are to die for." A woman giggled and her cohorts snorted.

Water ran in the sink. "I'm just glad Pastor Peterson's long sermon is over. He's good, but I wish he had a quicker delivery, shave off fifteen or twenty minutes."

"Hey, didn't his oldest daughter once have a thing going on with Carl?"

Sharonda stiffened.

"Why would he want *that* when he can have *this*?" Giggles. "Did you see what she's wearing? Those clothes. A fashion disaster. You'd think her mom would remind her we're approaching 2020, not The Roaring Twenties."

Who's out there? Sharonda burned to peep through the slit at the hinge of the door, but she couldn't afford to be spotted. She remained still.

"Believe me, her mother does try to help her, but Sharonda just doesn't care."

She'd grown up with that voice—Tina Smith lived on the same street. So much for neighborhood loyalty.

"First Lady Peterson is a different story. A real beauty in her day and still is. Pastor Peterson is like, what? Twelve years younger? But it's easy to see why he wanted *her*," Tina said.

Again, the obnoxious giggles. "They're an odd couple."

The automatic air freshener misted overhead, filling Sharonda's mouth with the taste of bitter florals. She flinched, bit her tongue, and prayed for them to leave before she gagged on the metallic taste of blood.

They left, but not before numbness settled in her legs. Sharonda exited the stall and stumbled to the sink. She rubbed at the sharp stinging behind her thighs and blinked against the moisture that blurred her vision. Refusing to touch anything her predecessors had, she twisted the nozzle with a handful of ripped pantyhose, then threw the worthless nylons at the nearby trashcan. Part hung over the top. She sighed, washed her hands, and rinsed her mouth. She stopped to stare at the water disappearing down the drain.

Oh, to disappear.

Sharonda palmed the sides of her face and pulled back. Her cheekbones strained to show. When she let go, they were lost again in the extra pounds collected in her cheeks. She dropped her gaze. Like the running faucet, tears ran free. She grabbed napkins, but not before ruining her camisole. Paper fibers covered her chest. Dusting the material only added more pieces. She yanked the lapels of her jacket close and jammed the top button through the hole to hide the mess. A quivered inhale sent the gold fastener in flight.

She gripped the edge of the basin and forced several deep breaths. Sharonda headed for the door, leaving the water on. She stopped and backtracked. "No need for both of us to be a waste." With one turn, she shut off the water and her emotions as best she could.

Back inside the sanctuary, Sharonda walked toward the front row. Her steps lagged. She slipped past women modeling big hats and thick-soled shoes, finding her customary place on the missionary pew next to Mother. Something about her magnolia fragrance became a balm to Sharonda's battered pride. She lifted her white lap scarf from the pew and sat. In what she hoped others would mistake as prayer, she bowed and studied the lace trim.

When the emcee turned the service over to Carl Ray, she looked up.

He sat at the keyboard.

Why was he here?

At the chorus of the well-known hymn, his soulful baritone drew Sharonda's complete attention.

Carl Ray held notes as if he didn't need a breath.

People swayed back and forth. Some shouted their praises, followed by sniffles. Claps. The bathroom ladies had gotten one piece of information correct. The eighteen-year-old recluse she'd known had morphed into a beautiful male specimen. And boy, could he sing!

Chills raised along her arms.

Mother nudged her and mouthed, *Stand up.*

Sharonda ignored her, even closed her eyes a moment, until Mother pinched her shoulder. She stood. Only after the reading of the Scripture did she sit. While she focused her eyes on the guest pastor, her mind traveled.

Dad hadn't mentioned Carl Ray. It couldn't have been part of the program because she'd attended the meetings. Planning today's event started a year ago. But much *had* changed since then.

"Amen," Sharonda chorused, not quite sure what she agreed to.

Dad probably called in a favor, and Carl Ray obliged after hearing how her brother's misconduct left them in a lurch. How long would Carl Ray be in town? Not that she planned to stick around and find out.

"Come. The altar is open." The pastor spread his arms wide.

Streams of people crowded the front of the church. Sharonda darted behind them and headed for the hallway to her father's office. Once inside the corridor, she stopped when she spotted a shapely set of legs accentuated by the highest pair of red-bottomed heels imaginable.

Sharonda kept her head lowered and allowed the brim of her hat to block the rest of the woman who stood in front of her.

"Sorry, can I help you?" Sharonda said.

"If you lose that hunched, broke-back shuffle you've adopted, you'd know it was me."

Sharonda raised her head and faced Janice. "What are *you* doing here?"

"You invited me." Her sister laughed.

"But you *never* accept my invitation. Why today?"

"I got a call from Tina Smith after the first service that *The* Carl Everhart is filling in as minister of music. Wasn't sure how you'd take the news. Thought you might need my support."

Sharonda shook her head. "He can't be Travis's replacement."

"He can. And is." Janice slipped her pumps off and carried them.

Sharonda fought to catch her breath. "He's back to *stay*?" She closed her eyes to ease her spinning head.

"Here, let me help you before you fall." Janice hurried her down the hall toward the only other room on the wing.

"Not there." Sharonda used the wall to help steady herself.

Janice struggled to get them both through the door. She dropped her shoes to hold Sharonda upright.

"Some help, please?"

Sharonda opened her eyes long enough to take in her surroundings. Sheets of music. A keyboard. Carl Ray.

Her girdle tightened. Half the room disappeared behind a black curtain. *Oh, Lord, please don't let me faint.* But like other times she'd asked Him for something, He didn't come through.

Chapter Three

Sharonda opened her eyes to rub the sting on her cheek. She sat in a chair, her upper body fully supported by her sister's hip.

Janice peered down and her hand hovered within striking distance of Sharonda's face. "That worked. You okay?"

"You hit me?" Sharonda straightened too fast. She flailed her arms to save herself from falling.

"I've got you." Carl Ray lifted Sharonda in one fluid motion.

She closed her eyes and buried her heated face against his chest as he carried her. Thank God his rich tone showed no sign of strain. Her tall, lanky boy of old had packed on muscle. She shifted from where his shirt button dug into her nose.

"You never answered your sister. Are you good?" He spoke so close, his bottom lip feathered her forehead.

Music pulsed in the background. "Who's playing?" Did she slur?

His scent. A sweet spice clung to his designer jacket.

She shook her head and forced her eyes open.

Carl Ray eased her onto the couch, positioning a pillow to support her head. "The stringed instruments are covering while the rest of us break."

Us? Derrick the drummer stood by the piano. "Oh."

Carl Ray knelt next to her. "Used the crowd as cover to escape, huh?"

"I-I ..." She clasped her hands together or else she'd smooth the lines from his brow by running the pads of her fingers over his high cheek bones, once littered with acne. Minimal scarring spotted his shaven face. "I'm fine."

Derrick approached. "You heard the woman. Stop smothering."

"Please run and get her a cold bottle of water."

"He thinks I'm his personal assistant." Derrick saluted Carl Ray then addressed Sharonda. "I don't know how many times I've requested a mini fridge for this room. If *you* ask, it'll get done." He winked and flashed Sharonda a huge grin, then left.

She smiled. "There's never a boring moment with him around."

"I'm going to go find Mother." Janice disappeared before Sharonda could say otherwise.

Carl stroked her moist temple. "You're too hot." He grabbed a sheet of music and fanned. "Don't you think warmer temperatures call for cooler clothes?"

Think? Pantyhose, girdle, half-slip to conceal the split in the skirt, while the full slip smoothed out the two humps where her breasts spilled over the top of her bra. Oh, the effort it took to complete the whole constricting creation. "Modesty comes at a price. It's not always comfortable."

"You scared me." He lowered the makeshift fan. "You'd tell me if something was wrong?" His gaze connected with hers, then softened.

She nodded.

He ran the back of his hand over her forehead and cupped her cheek. "Have you caught your breath?"

"Yes." She set every matured feature of his face to memory. Long lashes. Straight, broad nose. His full inviting mouth with lips that had always contrasted nicely with his light skin.

The door banged open.

They jumped.

"Boss man, break's over." Derrick handed the water bottle to Carl Ray, then hurried out again.

Sharonda pulled at her clothes. "Go. I'm fine. Janice and Mother are coming."

He pushed the paper fan into her hand, stood, and grabbed a music folder. "We'll talk tonight."

24

Sharonda swallowed. "What?"

"Yeah. Janice's idea. Like old times." He headed for the door but doubled back, the water still in his grasp. He handed her the drink and their fingers touched. He lingered.

Sharonda's cheeks warmed as she lifted her gaze from their hands to his face.

Mother rushed in with Janice. "Darling, I thought you fixed the problem this morning."

"Not now, Mother." She rubbed her hand down the front of her jacket. "Carl Ray, please go."

He turned. "First Lady. Janice." He acknowledged both women with a nod on his way out.

Sharonda refused to make eye contact with her mother.

"I see I must take matters in hand. Brice will be hearing from me. Today." She huffed. "Why are you holding your clothes that way?"

≈

The china sparkled under the chandelier's lighting. Sharonda filled Carl Ray's glass and sat the pitcher down on the formal dining table.

"Thank you. I haven't had a sit-down family meal in a long time," he said.

Stylish in his jacket and slacks from service, Carl Ray made her conscious of her brown linen pants, simple peasant top, and ponytailed hair.

"I thought as much." Janice bounced in her chair.

Across from Sharonda, Mother placed a juicy steak on Dad's plate.

"Thank you, love." Dad waved away her attempt to cut his meat. "I'm good. Eat." His gaze lingered on his wife's face as he patted her hand. The gesture seemed to settle the beginning of a pout.

Sharonda fiddled with the hem of her blouse.

"Carl, drink up. I made your favorite—Grape Kool-Aid." Mother rushed on, "Sharonda, the man's plate stands bare of bread. Hurry, child, pass the cornbread to Carl. He's a growing boy."

"Yes, ma'am." Sharonda wobbled the silver platter.

Carl Ray steadied the tray and rescued a square as it tumbled from the neat pyramid.

She stammered, "Thank you."

"You're welcome." He crumbled buttery bread over his cabbage.

Sharonda forked a candied yam and held it mid-air, distracted by Carl devouring his food. If only things had been different between them. Would he have consumed her cooking with such passion?

"Carl, it's been too long, brother." Janice batted her long lashes. "I'm glad you were able to join us."

Sharonda gripped her fork.

"Missed you too, peanut."

"Really? Then explain all the letters and phone calls we *never* received?" Janice gave him the perfect pouty lips.

"I called." He added a dash of pepper sauce to his cabbage. "Ask Sharonda."

Everyone faced her.

"I called more when I first left. Later on, sporadically." Carl wiped his mouth with a napkin. "Well, whenever my schedule permitted. But in the last six months I couldn't get her to return my calls. Maybe I should've written." Carl smiled at Sharonda.

She plugged her mouth with the cold candied yam and stabbed another one on her plate.

Mother angled toward Janice. "Seeing you at church blessed this old lady's soul." Her matronly voice grew animated.

Janice groaned.

"It's all the missionaries talked about after service. I'm so glad you came. You should come more often. How lovely you looked in that beautiful blue dress. So put together. Sharonda ought to take notes." She leaned toward her youngest child. "I so miss your being there. Maybe you and Carl can sing a selection now that he's back." Her eyes shined.

Sharonda cringed. They *would* make a beautiful couple.

"Broddrick, you did mention to Carl the possibility of the position becoming permanent?" Mother quickened her words. "*Temporary* works my nerves. You know how I hate change. I'm at a stage in life where permanence is a must." She retrieved a fresh napkin and set it beside Father's plate. "You *know* how I hate change. With Travis not returning my calls, I'm not sure I can stand much more."

Dad took Mother's hand between his. "Breathe, dear, you're repeating yourself. It's not good for you to become overexcited."

Mother's emotions seemed to crash against an invisible shoreline. Tide in. She calmed and sipped her tea. Tide out.

Sharonda released a ragged breath and clasped her hands together in her lap.

Carl Ray blanketed Sharonda's trembling fingers. She held on to the strength he offered. He'd always been there for her family. For her. The corners of her eyes stung.

Dad lulled Mother into a conversation that seemed to soothe her.

Janice leaned forward, exposing the swell of her chest. "Carl, you know I want the scoop. Do tell why you accepted the *short-term* position at New Hope."

Had her voice become sultry? Sharonda glanced at Carl Ray.

"What would you like to know?" He smiled as he rubbed his thumb over the back of Sharonda's hand.

"Everything." Janice ran an acrylic nail along the rim of her glass.

If her sister decided she wanted Carl Ray, he wouldn't be able to resist. Sharonda pulled away from him and gripped her water glass.

"Sharonda, you okay?" Carl Ray nodded toward her plate. "Why aren't you eating?"

"What? You think all I do is sit around and eat?" Her last few words rushed out as a sharp cramp seized her side.

Carl's jaw twitched.

"What's going on?" Mother dropped her conversation with Dad.

Sharonda stared at her food.

"All is well, Lady Peterson." Carl Ray turned to face Janice. "Staying at the folks' house since having the emergency appendectomy, but you probably knew that. Suffered infections. The extended recovery kept me from going on tour." He sipped his drink. "I was at the end of my contract. Didn't feel led to go into another. At least not right away."

"So, Coleen and Gregg came in from the mission fields to care for you?" Mother said.

Carl Ray choked on his Kool-Aid. He put the glass down and tapped his chest a couple times. "My parents haven't looked after me in a long time. I had home-care nurses. Couldn't have pulled through without them."

He could've died.

Sharonda forked elbow noodles. She counted nine green beans and squirmed in her seat. Anything to keep from reaching out to him.

"I didn't mean to pry." Mother blotted the corners of her mouth.

"So, it's not true?" Janice sulked. "I heard you were putting in a guest performance at the Gospel Stage Play at the community theater this Saturday."

He grinned. "Where did you hear that?"

Sharonda speared the green vegetables and transferred them to the right.

"That's for me to know. Now, out with it." Janice sashayed around the table. "Yes or no?" She pulled on his arm until she held his hand.

Carl Ray pulled free. "Let's just say I'm helping out an old buddy."

"Your secret is safe with me." Janice hugged him from behind; her breasts pressed against his back. "Why not help me with a couple tickets?"

Carl Ray leaned forward.

Janice released him and stood to his side, planting herself between him and Sharonda. She placed her hands on her hips. "You gonna hook your girl up?"

"No promises, but I'll see if Bonner has any to spare."

Sharonda tapped her fork against the edge of her plate.

"Janice, sit down. You're at the table. You've been trained better." Mother fanned her face with her napkin.

Janice folded her arms and grunted.

"You heard your mother." Father pushed his plate forward. "I tell you what, run to the store and pick up some ice cream to go with the chocolate cake."

"But I need to talk with Carl," Janice whined but moved toward her chair.

28

Sharonda cracked her knuckles. If that had been her.

"Sharonda Lorraine Peterson!" Mother fisted her hand. "Only men pop their joints in such a crass manner. You weren't raised in a barn."

"Sorry, Mother." Sharonda clutched the sides of her seat. She fought the urge to look in Carl Ray's direction when he squeezed her elbow. She pulled away from his touch.

He laid his fork by his plate. "Peanut, I'm not leaving town anytime soon. We'll catch up."

"Sharonda, won't you be a dear and run to the store and get the ice cream?" Janice's syrupy sweetness set her teeth on edge. "You can take my car."

Father stood. "I told *you*—"

"It's all right." Sharonda pushed back from the table. "I don't mind."

Dad sat.

Carl Ray didn't belong to her. Janice could take him.

On her way out, she slammed the door leading to the garage.

≈

Arms laden with two grocery bags, Sharonda struggled to open the door. She entered the kitchen from the garage.

"Let me take that." Carl Ray lifted the damp sack with the ice cream before she could warn him. The bottom gave, sending groceries to the floor.

Sharonda scrambled to collect candy, cheesy puffs, and random chocolates. "What are you doing in the kitchen?"

Carl Ray placed the tub of homemade vanilla in the sink and returned to gather more items. "I heard the garage door, and I wanted to see if you needed any help."

They both reached for the cookie dough and raised their heads at the same time.

"Ouch!" She rubbed her crown. "Lately, I've become a total klutz."

He massaged his chin. "I have to be more careful. I'm going to stop helping before you have to visit the hospital." He held her gaze. "I'm sorry."

29

Did he refer to the head bump? Somehow, she didn't think so. She stashed the bag of chips and candies into the one sack. "Where's everybody? My sister?" She crossed to the fridge, placed the dough on the shelf, and stuffed her snacks into the bottom drawer.

"Your mother was tired. Your dad escorted her to rest. Janice went to change clothes."

"You two have made plans? A date?" She pivoted to leave. "Don't mind me. Let me get out of here so you and Janice can have your privacy. Good night." She glanced at the closed refrigerator door, then headed across the kitchen.

"Sharonda, wait. What can I do to fix things between us? I hate—"

"Don't." She stopped and turned to face him. "You don't get it, do you?" She closed the distance between them. "Just because you have regrets doesn't mean I do."

He reached out.

She stepped back to avoid contact. "If you want to say you hated kissing me ..." Sharonda swallowed the lump forming in her throat. "If you want to say you hated telling me how beautiful I was ..." Her voice faded to a whisper. "If you regret making love to me ..." She shook her head. "Don't."

He reached and caressed her cheek. "Please, let me explain."

Why did it feel so natural to lean into his touch? She shook her head. "No." Sharonda crossed her arms.

His fingers kneaded the tops of her shoulders as he pulled her to his chest. Carl's strong embrace and the familiar spice seduced her arms to fall limp at her sides. He stroked her ponytail. "You deserved more."

Brice. The reality of her future caused her to push away. "I didn't have any remorse then, and I don't *now.*"

He winced.

She stepped around Carl Ray on her way to the refrigerator, snagged her treats, then ripped open the chips. She stuffed two in her mouth at once.

"Sharonda."

She spun around to face him and wiped cheesy fingers on her pants. "Good night." She held up the puffs. "Like you, I've got a date."

Chapter Four

Carl Ray stuck the vanilla ice cream in the freezer and closed the door. He pressed his forehead against the refrigerator's smooth surface and groaned. Why hadn't he chased after her? Not until Sharonda walked out of the kitchen—replacing him with a bag of chips—did he realize he wanted to do more than apologize. Covering her trembling hands at the table? Second nature.

Like his desire to protect her. Defend her.

"Carl?"

He turned to face Janice.

She crossed the room in a long flowing dress—a beautiful red that complimented her chocolate complexion. The silk plunged and billowed over every curve. Guesswork, eliminated.

"Why the long face?" She ran her hand over his shoulder.

He tensed as he remembered the women prowling backstage after a performance. "Peanut, you sure could learn from your sister. Less is more—leave some things for a man's imagination."

"A peek never killed anybody." Janice fluttered a hand over her revealing cleavage.

Carl looked away.

She placed her palm on his cheek and turned him to face her again. "Hey, what's wrong? What's with the frown?" The lustful sensuality in her body language reeked of the same worldly confidence he'd once lived.

"I'm good." Carl sidestepped to the sink.

"Hey, you?" Janice snapped her fingers. "What happened while I was gone?" She stepped toward him.

He leaned back. "Sharonda thinks we're a couple. Or at least, that's what she implied before she stormed off to her bedroom with *her* date."

"Date?" Janice lifted her brow.

"Chester Cheetah, himself. The way Sharonda stuffed her mouth with those cheesy puffs made me wish I'd been invited. She didn't appear to be in the mood to share."

Janice laughed. "Sorry, that's not funny, but it is."

"Nothing's funny about Sharonda's believing a lie." The words escaped louder than he expected. Carl lifted both hands. "Forgive me for raising my voice."

She looked down toward her black pointed pumps and toed the grout in the tiled floor. "It's not your fault. I may have taken my flirting a little too far tonight."

"Flirting? With who?"

"It doesn't do a girl's pride any good to learn the object of her affections didn't notice her attention." She looked up and held his gaze.

Carl raised his brow. "Me?"

"Yes, you." Janice pursed her lips. "I, uh." She tugged at her dress to diminish the cleavage. "Know what happened between you and my sister."

That came out of nowhere. He gripped the back of his neck, fighting the urge to look away. "Can you be more specific?"

"It was the same day Mom made her try on the new dancewear in front of the praise dance team. 'Too much of a distraction,' Mom said. You saw the pictures. She was way more developed than the others, a sure way to earn a couple haters."

He shoved sweaty palms into his pants pockets but held her gaze.

"Even after the other parents had the girls delete the images from their phones, the incident spread to anyone who would watch. Or laugh." She clasped her hands in front of her. "I thought we were alone in the house. You and Travis were supposed to be playing basketball somewhere

34

in the neighborhood. I went to the bedroom to check on Sharonda. I heard you." Janice dipped her chin. "Saw you when you slipped out."

"I'm sorry," he said.

"Don't be. Everybody's human. I never told." Janice ran a hand over the flowing fabric of her dress, down her sides, and brushed imaginary wrinkles. "But she changed."

An ache gripped his chest.

Janice shrugged. "This holier-than-thou routine Sharonda's adopted is getting old. That's why I sent you the job posting for the Minister of Music interim position. I just want my sister back. Happy and *holy* if that's what it'll take."

"Wait, you sent the email? I don't understand."

"Heated discussions are becoming a regular occurrence around here. And it pays to have an ear at the church. I simply made sure your email address made the list Dad sent to his secretary. The rest was news to me. Maybe I should try my hand at gambling. Or there might be something to this God stuff." She tossed long curls over her shoulder. "Deep down inside, I believe you looked for a way back to Sharonda. Why else would you answer that post?" Janice uncrossed her arms. "There has to be more to life than what I've seen. More to it than Sharonda dragging through the motions every day. And if my family wants me to sign on to their beliefs, their way of life, I have to see there's something good in this thing for Sharonda." Her shoulders deflated. "And me."

Carl paced. Little sisters grew up emulating the older sibling. But no, his own actions contributed to Sharonda not being the person Janice needed.

Father, what have I done? He lowered his gaze to Janice. He nodded to encourage her to continue.

"Sharonda has lived her life inside a cocoon, pretending nothing matters but hurt by everything. Tonight, something changed. The robotic Sharonda disappeared. When she thought I might be moving in on you, her eyes shot flames." Janice swayed her hips. "I'm glad you weren't interested in my little act." She narrowed her eyes. "I need you to be honest with me. Did you use my sister back then, or did she mean something to you?"

He closed the distance. "I may not have truly loved her then, but I wish I had."

Janice touched his forearm. "So, you're going to make it right?" Hope shone in her eyes, giving Carl a glimpse of the little girl he'd grown up with.

"I'm not sure it's that easy. First I have to figure out what *right* is in this situation."

She planted both hands against his chest and pushed with enough force, he stepped back. "How is it you church folk spout all this talk about power and heaven, but here on Earth, you're helpless?" Janice walked toward the back door. She flicked her hair out of her face as she looked back at Carl. "Sharonda's birthday is in three days. Get me those tickets, and you'll have your chance to start figuring things out. If anybody asks, tell them I've gone out with some friends. They don't need to wait up."

≈

Please, let me explain. Snippets of last night's conversation with Carl Ray infiltrated Sharonda's thoughts. She pumped her legs and arms. Her heartbeat pulsed in her ears; she didn't want to stop. She slowed, struggling to catch her breath after the sprint interval. Her legs burned.

Sharonda stepped onto the curb and perspiration dripped into her eyes. She wiped her face with the towel draped around her neck. At the sound of a car's approach, she turned.

Dad looked so good behind the lowered window of his black Mercedes. "You want a ride?" He appeared refreshed from his morning prayer time at the church.

"I'm ..." Sharonda entered into a coughing fit.

Dad parked and rushed to her side. "Breathe in. Out." Her father lifted her arms. "Don't try to talk just yet. Walking wouldn't do all this. Did you run? Don't answer that. Through the nose. Out the mouth." Father's confident cadence added a sense of security.

36

Finally, her breathing matched her father's calming strokes to her back. "I'm good, Dad."

"You sure?" He knit his brow together.

Sharonda wanted to wrap her arm through his for added support but she refrained. Too sweaty. Besides, Dad had never been comfortable with open affection, especially in public.

"Let's get you in the car."

She slouched into the passenger seat. The joints in her knees screamed their relief.

"You can't start out running. Does this sudden motivation to exercise have anything to do with Carl's return?"

Sharonda coughed again. "I didn't run long. Off and on." She wheezed out her words. "Sweat suit—bad decision in this Texas heat. I may have pushed too hard. Forgot water."

"Are you avoiding the question?" He increased the air conditioner. Sharonda extended her hands toward the vent, took a deep breath, then exhaled. Her heart no longer felt like it would beat out of her chest. "Don't you think I need to lose some weight?"

"Becoming healthy is one thing. Out to kill yourself is another." Dad pulled into the garage and parked next to the empty bay reserved for Mother's pearl-white Lexus.

Sharonda held the door handle. "But if I lost weight ..."

Dad shut the motor off. "You're doing so well. Don't lose your head over Carl. When he's back on his feet, he'll return to the fast life. His life's in New York, not Longview. Brice is more your type."

She struggled to swallow. Not you too, Daddy? "Oh? So what's Carl Ray's type?"

He shrugged. "He's young. Handsome. Talented. Popular with the ladies. I have to admit he seems to have matured since he left, but he's *still* a man. I remember that age. Brice is older with fewer distractions. He can appreciate the average life."

"Is that how you see me?" Sharonda whispered. "Average?"

"That's not what I meant." He glanced into the rearview mirror even though they sat in the garage.

"Really, Daddy?" Sharonda blinked through blurred vision.

He turned toward her. "You must understand, most men in their youth are out to fulfill the lusts of the flesh. They're selfish and will manipulate to lie with anybody." He reached for her hand. "My girls have a rare beauty. Inside and out."

She scrambled through old memories, trying to recall a time her father had ever told her she was beautiful. "Your mother wouldn't approve," he'd told her at a birthday party when she reached for a second helping of her favorite chocolate cake. "Magna cum laude," he'd bragged at church. He even hugged her the day she received her master's degree. But never the word beautiful. No, that was reserved for Janice.

"Sharonda?"

She pulled her hand away and leaned against the car door. "By saying they will lie with anybody, do you mean those of us who are *average*? Or were you hoping a few more pounds would keep them away?" No wonder he'd never defended her against Mother's rants over how she dressed and ate. "Don't answer." So much for being a daddy's girl. She yanked the door handle and stumbled out.

"Sharonda, I didn't say that," he called from inside the car.

"I think you've said enough." She slammed the door, then hurried to her room. Would she ever be enough for anyone?

Chapter Five

Daddy, Mother, and Janice sang happy birthday from the entrance of her bathroom. Her sister held the cupcake; a single candle burned at the center.

The longer they sang, the more Sharonda struggled to stay mad at her family. She twisted the cold-water nozzle and rinsed the blue mouthwash down the sink before she faced the trio. "You shouldn't have. Thirty is too old to celebrate birthdays like this." She maneuvered around them to leave the bathroom and crossed to her side of the room.

"Be grateful your parents are alive to serenade you. My father started the tradition and I *will* keep it going," Mother said.

The small caravan followed close on her heels. Daddy moved to stand at his wife's side and rubbed her back.

"Come on already, before wax melts all over everything." Janice raised the cupcake in her direction.

"Blow out your candle, baby." Dad's eyes glistened.

Had he thought about their last encounter? For the last few days, she wasn't sure if he'd avoided her or if she'd avoided him. She puckered and blew. "There. Now you can leave. I'm sure you all have better things to do."

Mother dismissed her with a wave. "Oh, Sharonda, stop it. You act as if we don't do something every year for our children's birthdays. I remember getting you the membership to the new 24 Hour Fitness center last year." She turned, making her yellow maxi dress flare out as she walked to the bathroom.

Sharonda bit her tongue to silence a comeback.

Janice handed the cake to Dad. "A membership? I would've forgotten too."

"I got your favorite." Dad nodded toward the cupcake. "Red velvet?" His gaze lifted high enough to hold hers.

A peace offering. She was sure he'd suffered to present the sweet treat. Forever monitoring her calories, Mother had exchanged the customary birthday cake for a fruit bouquet years ago. Sharonda chewed her lip to stop it from quivering.

Although dysfunctional, they were family.

Mother sashayed out of the bathroom. "Stop the waterworks, child— makes the eyes all red and puffy. Why didn't you tell me you got your period? No wonder you've been cloistered in your room."

Sharonda wiped her face with the arm of her robe. "Mother!" Intense heat torched her cheeks. Might as well serve them up as a regular crème brûlée. "Were you snooping around my bathroom?"

"Hosh-posh. My house. My bathroom. I can't snoop something that belongs to me. Just observant." Mother dropped a white envelope into the front pocket of Sharonda's robe. "Janice is taking you shopping. There's enough money to buy something nice and have a healthy lunch at Glam Ma's Eatery. Especially after consuming that junk." She scowled at the cupcake but quickly turned a smile toward Dad. "See, honey, she's fine. You've gotten worked up for nothing. This explains the emotional outbursts of late. Sharonda has the constitution of ten oxen."

Leave it to her mother to excuse their behavior with some shortcoming or diagnosis attributed to the wounded party. Her dad *should* feel bad for his hurtful words.

Janice stepped closer and waved two strips of paper in her face. "Happy birthday, sis. You won't believe what I got you. Correction, Carl Ray got you tickets to his performance."

Carl Ray? "You asked him for tickets to his play for my birthday?"

"What else would I be getting them for?" Janice lifted one side of her brow.

Sharonda pulled the sash tighter around her waist. Did she misjudge her sister's actions at dinner with Carl Ray? "Thank you."

Janice pinched Sharonda's cheek and slipped one of the two tickets in her other robe pocket. "I may have taken my dramatics a little too far the other evening, but never doubt my motives when it comes to you. I love you."

"Forgive me," Sharonda said.

Janice gave a thumbs-up and a wink.

"What's all this talk about Carl getting tickets? Did he send one for Brice?" Mother seemed to inspect the top of Sharonda's dresser. "Is there something I need to know?"

Sharonda wrapped her arms around herself. "Brice is still in revival."

"As long as you understand *your* commitments." Mother rearranged the items on the dresser.

"Don't worry, Mother. *I* understand."

Daddy turned Mother toward the door while balancing the cupcake in the other hand. "Let's take our little party to the kitchen and let Sharonda get dressed." He draped his arm around her. Mother leaned against his side as they walked out of the bedroom.

Janice followed.

Sharonda lifted an accent pillow from her bed and screamed. She couldn't live another year the same—things had to change. She flung the pillow on the floor, picked up the black dress she'd laid out, and headed back to her closet. She stepped into her faithful cross trainers, exchanged the robe for a denim skirt after transferring her gifts from the pockets, and slid a flower-patterned V-neck cotton shirt over her head.

Today, she'd see Carl Ray perform on stage—a dream come true. And she'd be fashionable for the event. Sharonda left the closet and closed the door behind her.

Daddy had remembered her favorite flavor. She smiled.

⌐⌐

The auditorium buzzed with excited chatter. It seemed as if everyone in Longview had decided to spend their Saturday evening at the community theater for the gospel stage play.

"I'm so glad you picked out my outfit. Except for the heels." Sharonda linked her arm with Janice to walk down the crowded aisle.

"Flats are for girls. Tonight is special." Janice giggled. "You would've come in your Sunday's best, looking like one of the mothers of the church." She nodded toward a group of older ladies in the audience.

Sharonda couldn't protest. One wore a replica of the gray skirt and suit jacket hanging in her closet. She tugged the wide belt, cinching the waistline of the new, calf-length pencil skirt and endless ruffle blouse.

Time spent with Janice's friend Tawni Haynes, owner of the custom dress shop specializing in plus sizes, had been worth every minute. She appreciated the way the shop owner rifled through her entire ready-to-wear pieces until she found something Sharonda liked. Something that made her feel beautiful.

Someone grabbed Sharonda's free hand. "Hey, you looking for a seat?" A man, probably a couple years younger than her father, flashed his gold front tooth and winked.

"No, thank you, sir." She jerked away at the same time Janice pulled. Sharonda struggled to keep from toppling her sister. "I can't believe he did that."

"I can." Music cued and Janice navigated them through the crowd toward the stage. "You look stunning, sis."

Sharonda spoke close to her sister's ear. "Your friend picked the perfect outfit."

"I'm not talking about the clothes." Janice squeezed Sharonda's bicep. "I haven't seen you like this in a long while. There's a twinkle in your eyes. Today was fun, like old times."

Sharonda smiled. "I love you, too."

They slid past people—apologized for bumping knees—until they reached the two empty seats on the third row, center.

The house lights lowered and announcements boomed through the speakers. Soon, a talented group of actors pulled Sharonda into *You are Your Brother's Keeper*, a twisted tale of love and redemption.

She heard him before he appeared, as if he'd come from heaven to deliver the message. Adorned with wings and a white robe, Carl Ray sang the words of an old hymn to the desperate pastor stretched out over the altar of the church set.

Sharonda imagined herself in the place of the pastor—kneeling to unload the burdens of her heart and her fears. If only she could believe He really cared.

Janice's fingers intertwined hers and tightened.

She wiped her cheeks and sat on the edge of her seat until the audience jumped to their feet and clapped. Sharonda joined them.

"Let's go," Janice yelled as she pulled her arm.

"Where are we going?" Sharonda stumbled after she stomped someone's foot.

"Ouch!" The elderly lady on the end frowned at her.

Sharonda winced. "I'm so sorry."

"Carl said to get to the side door as quick as possible." Janice tugged her forward. They joined three people to the left of the stage.

"Why are we lining up?"

"Not we. *You.*" Janice gave her a quick side hug and handed her another ticket. "You have a backstage pass to spend an hour with your favorite performer." She kissed Sharonda's cheek, then disappeared into the crowd.

"Janice. Wait," Sharonda called over the growing noise. Strangers bumped and shoved her, forcing her to face forward in the line.

A young lady with cherry-stained lips said something.

"Huh?" Sharonda shook her head.

Wearing a bright orange pants suit, the woman showcased her generous, sparkling cleavage and small waist. She leaned, cupped her hands around Sharonda's ear, and yelled, "How did *you* get a gold ticket?"

Sharonda stepped back and brushed nervous hands over the skirt. She matched the stranger's volume, "My sister got the ticket for me."

"You want to trade? My pass is for the lead actor, but you seem more the pastor's type. If I'd known Carl Everhart was the guest vocalist, I would've made sure he knew *I* was in attendance. Carl and I go way back. I've been a fan for years."

Sharonda cinched her belt tighter. Her father's words crushed her afresh. *Carl's not your type.* Not even her new clothes combated her deflating confidence. She examined the ticket she held.

The buxom beauty snatched the golden strip away. "You'll enjoy the pastor. It's rumored that he'll show you a good time."

Chapter Six

Lights, applause, and people rose to their feet with shouts and whistles. Carl used to live for such a response, but tonight, he focused on Janice who kept a firm hold on Sharonda's arm. She pulled her toward the right of the orchestra pit where the VIP ticket holders gathered.

Carl anticipated Sharonda joining him backstage so he could share his world. One that he'd wanted her to be a part of for a long time.

She wrung her hands, making the golden voucher sparkle like a diamond under the lights. Then, Sharonda passed the ticket to the woman in the mandarin orange jumpsuit. The same woman who'd been hanging around at every practice.

Pain exploded in Carl's shoulder as Aaron, his bass guitarist and the pastor in the play, yanked his arm to bow. "Not so rough."

"You weren't responding to the knuckle squeeze. Had to do something." Aaron bowed again, working the crowd into another round of boisterous applause.

Forced to take his eyes off Sharonda, Carl bent at his waist, then rose. He scanned the surrounding area. *Where's Janice?* The curtain closed.

He rushed to the stairs.

"Good job, Carl."

He didn't break his stride to see who spoke.

"Can I have your autograph?" A gray-headed lady pressed paper and pen into his hands the moment Carl reached the floor.

He scribbled and thrust the signed paper back.

"Can I get a picture?"

"Sorry." Carl kept walking in the direction of Sharonda.

"Jerk."

He couldn't stop to make amends.

The fan pressed a silver ticket in Sharonda's hand and turned as Carl approached. Her jumpsuit exposed a glitter-bedazzled chest.

"What's going on here?" He searched Sharonda's face for an answer. Her eyes filled with unshed tears.

"Carl." The other woman moved close and palmed his chest with a familiarity she hadn't earned.

He stepped back. "Excuse me?"

"Don't act like you don't *know* me." She raised her voice.

"Recognizing a fan's face from hanging around the set is not the same as knowing someone."

She recoiled.

Sharonda moved away from them, shaking her head.

"It's not what you think." Carl reached out and his fingers grazed her blouse.

Sharonda slipped away from his grasp and bumped into Aaron.

"Second Lady Peterson, I see you purchased a ticket for a backstage experience with the pastor." Aaron grinned and draped his arm over Sharonda's shoulders.

"I didn't" Sharonda looked from the ticket she held to the woman next to Carl. "She gave it to me."

"No, we traded." The fan leaned toward Carl. "Seeing how you and I go way back. *She* agreed we weren't matched properly. Take my word, the pastor here"—she smirked in Aaron's direction—"gives a girl her money's worth."

Carl closed the distance between him and Aaron. He forced words past a rigid jaw. "I can't imagine a *married* man doing what she just implied."

Aaron dropped his arm from around Sharonda's shoulder. "I'm not sure what you *think* she implied. Are you speaking from experience?"

Carl redirected his attention. "Sharonda, how can you give away a birthday gift?" He pulled the golden strip from the fan girl's hand. "Maybe you'd like to spend your evening with Aaron and that's fine with me, but your sister set this up. And your parents are expecting *me* to bring you home." He glared at the guitarist.

Aaron raised his hands in surrender. "Hey, Tomeka is an old friend. I'm just trying to take care of my fans. So, who's here to use my ticket?"

The three focused on Sharonda.

She shrugged and lifted the silver strip. Her hand shook. "I'm sorry for the confusion. My sister sprung this backstage visit on me at the last second."

Carl took the silver strip from her grasp. "Let's get you home." He turned to Aaron and handed him the voucher. "I'd suggest you do the same."

Aaron narrowed his eyes. "You forget yourself. We're not at the church." He turned to Tomeka and smiled. "I believe I owe you a tour."

She let her gaze travel Aaron's body from head to toe, straightened her spine, and flashed a toothy grin. "That you do, Pastor."

Aaron extended his arm to Tomeka. "Shall we?"

"Yes, we shall." She giggled.

⌇

Sharonda looked out the car window as Carl Ray drove past Burlington's on Judson Road. "Why are we headed north?"

"For someone ready to take a tour with the pastor, I didn't think you were in a rush to get home."

"I wasn't." She folded her arms. "Never mind."

He slowed as they approached the light. "No explanation needed. You're a grown woman."

"You obviously have another engagement. Someone else would've given me a ride home," she said.

"Like Aaron?" He turned right to The Summit Club and parked. He shut off the engine and faced her.

"Really? A married man?" Sharonda turned her head, refusing to look at him. "Take me home."

47

"Demanding aren't we?" He huffed. "Playing the role of the spoiled daughter. Isn't that the baby sister's role?"

"You tell me." She unbuckled her seatbelt to turn toward him. "The two of you have spent a lot of time together recently."

"No more than I've spent with you." Carl Ray looked out the windshield and gripped the steering wheel. "This is the play's reception dinner. Ten minutes, and I'll get you home. Can you spare the time?"

She frowned. "Why are you upset?"

"I'm good."

"Liar."

He angled toward her. "Why did you trade my ticket?"

"You think I did so *willingly*? That woman insisted y'all went way back. What was I supposed to do?"

"Fight for me. The way you used to." The uncertainty in his eyes took her back to their high school days when they did fight for each other. Protected one another. "I didn't know the mandarin stalker's name until Aaron called her Tomeka. She's been hanging around since rehearsals started."

"Mandarin stalker?"

"That orange suit." He crossed his eyes, making gag noises. "Over the top."

They both laughed.

He covered her hand on the middle console. "Let's get in there so I can drive you home."

Sharonda reached for the door.

He squeezed her fingers. "Wait for me."

She swallowed. That's all she'd been doing. Until Brice.

Carl Ray hurried to open her door. "At your service." He extended a hand.

Sharonda accepted.

"Hold up." His arm snagged around her waist. "You have something on your chin. Look toward the light."

She lifted her head.

Carl Ray rubbed his thumb beneath her lip. Lingered.

She whispered. "What?"

"You're so beautiful."

"Yeah, right." Sharonda dropped her chin and glanced toward the entrance.

"Stop. You look great. I don't understand what you meant by that last statement, but I didn't like it. You're perfect the way God made you."

They reached the entrance and Carl Ray halted and spoke close to her ear. "There's nothing between me and Janice but brotherly affection toward a sister. Tonight ... was supposed to be about you and your birthday."

"It's been a great day. The play. You were wonderful."

"But you missed your backstage tour."

"Everything worked out." She chewed her lower lip to keep from finishing her thought. *When I'm with you, nothing else matters.* Sharonda pulled him closer to allow another couple to enter the building. "I went to see you." She lifted her chin, waited, and willed Carl Ray to understand how much he meant to her. *Brice.* Her conscience screamed. She lowered her gaze. "I need to tell you something."

He placed a gentle finger on her lips. "Back in the day, you didn't have to tell me your thoughts, I knew them. Twelve years is a long time. I've gotten rusty, my friend." *Friend.* He might as well have dumped a bucket of ice water over her head.

He kissed her forehead. "After you." Carl Ray opened the door.

Inside, white accented the walls and tables as thousands of tiny lights twinkled. Orchids, peony, white hydrangea, and sweet peas overflowed in vases around the room. The names of some of the smaller floral sprigs eluded her. Massive centerpieces, in their elegant array, stood tall overlooking the gold-trimmed table settings for eight. A hint of candied citrus filled the air. To their left, a live band played jazz.

Sharonda whispered, "Wow."

Carl Ray stroked her hair. "There're so many things I'd love to witness through your eyes."

She tilted her head. "You sound sad. How can anyone be sad surrounded by so many admirers?"

"Admiration can be fickle. Learned that the hard way." He secured her hand in the crook of his arm, then steered her toward an older couple at the head table. "Mr. Wisener, I'd like to introduce you to Sharonda Peterson."

"Carl! Wonderful performance." The man stood—his head even with Carl Ray's chin—and gave a dismissive wave toward the tiny woman next to him. He adjusted the bow tie around his thick neck. "Wish you were local. The ladies love you. Ticket sales don't lie, and for every man present, there were seven women filling those seats."

"People respond to a good message." A sharpness entered Carl Ray's voice.

"Aww, being modest, I see. But I know what sells, and it had everything to do with the church's pretty boy." The little man pounded Carl on his shoulder. "I know you performed as a favor to your old friend, Pastor Bonner, but contact my production company next time you're in town. I can make it worth your while."

"Excuse us." Carl Ray nodded to the man's wife. "Have a pleasant evening. Church in the morning." He pulled Sharonda away.

"How rude." She gripped his arm to keep from stumbling.

Carl Ray slowed once again and covered her hand with his. "Sorry about that. This is the business side of performing I wish I could avoid. A few more rounds should do it."

They strolled through the room, shaking hands.

After introductions to so many different faces, Sharonda lagged behind and found a seat. She kneaded the strain in her lower back.

Carl Ray retrieved her from her hiding place. He offered her his hand and pulled her up into an embrace. "No more. Let's go." His warm breath rushed over her earlobe. He nestled her hand in the crook of his arm and whisked her toward the exit.

"Carl Ray Everhart." A long-haired black Barbie swooped in between them.

One moment, Sharonda was connected to his arm and the next, she stood alone.

The woman wrapped her arms around Carl Ray's waist. She pressed against his side as if they'd been paired and packaged to fit inside a narrow shoe box. She was everything Sharonda wasn't—tall, slender, and in control.

"This is Sharonda Peterson." Carl beckoned to her.

She smiled having forgotten the woman's name. "You're drop-dead gorgeous."

The woman appeared to study Sharonda. "Where did you find her? She's cute, Carl." She ran her long fingers down his arm.

Oh, my feet hurt. Sharonda balanced her weight on one leg as she tapped the heel of her right foot first, then the other, to relieve some of the strain. She turned away from their conversation. Too familiar with the mean girl routine, Sharonda didn't wait to hear the "but" that was sure to follow. *Cute face for a big girl, but ...* She'd heard it one too many times.

During the ride home, she reclined in the passenger seat, closed her eyes, and tuned out the world.

Carl Ray nudged her shoulder. "Hey, you."

Sharonda lifted a heavy head to see the thick cedar beams at the entryway of her house.

"Yep."

Once again, he took her hand as she stepped from the truck and lifted her chin until she looked into his eyes. "What's wrong?"

"Nothing." She tucked a strand of hair behind her ear. "I had fun. Thanks."

He stroked the side of her face. "You sure?"

She covered his hand for a moment. "It should be well after midnight, way past my bedtime."

"But you had something you wanted to talk about."

More like someone. "It can wait." She turned toward the house.

He pulled her to face him again. "And I've waited too long to speak my piece."

51

"No," Sharonda shook her head and darted toward the house. She stumbled and snapped one heel of her new shoes. No big loss. Flats worked better in her average life anyway.

A car door slammed behind her.

"Come on, Sharonda. Why are you running from me?"

She turned and pointed her broken shoe at him. "No."

He stopped.

"Good night." She hobbled inside.

Carl rushed and placed his hand on the doorjamb. "Sharonda. Don't shut me out. Tell me how to fix things between us."

"I didn't realize anything was broken." She pushed at his fingers until he pulled away long enough for her to close and lock the door. With her back against the entrance, she covered her face with her hands.

At the sound of his truck leaving, she sank to the floor.

I can't be your friend.

Chapter Seven

Sharonda shut off the vacuum. She'd have sworn someone crashed cymbals outside. She glanced at the grandfather clock. 9:00 p.m.

She walked to the window overlooking the iron patio furniture into her neighbor's back yard. No signs of trouble. Stars twinkled in a clear sky. Sharonda loosened the sash so the drapes fluttered closed, shutting out the darkness. Maybe her ears played tricks. Anytime she couldn't hear over the hum of the vacuum, she imagined strangers coming in on her unawares. She huffed. *Stop being silly.* Sharonda crossed the area rug.

Clanging sounded from the kitchen.

She rounded the corner and bumped into Dad.

"You okay?" He steadied her.

"Yes, sir." She glanced around. "Did you hear that?" Sharonda stepped behind him as they headed toward the kitchen. He could handle an intruder if one entered through the garage.

Every bottom row cabinet door stood open. Pots and pans littered the floor. Others were piled in the sink with suds spilling over the sides. Mother stood in the middle of the mess.

"Marianne?" Dad said.

She turned and soapy water dripped from the pot she held. Dark wet patches covered the front of her cotton shirt.

Dad approached. "Marianne, honey, what are you doing?" He attempted to remove the pan from her only to have his hands slapped.

Sharonda gripped the doorjamb.

Mother tugged at the rubber glove on her right hand. "Don't *honey* me. I've waited on you long enough. If things are going to be cleaned up around here, it's up to *me*."

"Sharonda cleaned the kitchen after dinner." Dad clasped his hands behind his back and spoke in calm tones.

"I'm referring to the stuff people hide in corners and crevices, collecting dust. You leave secrets covered long enough, and they're uncovered when you least expect it. Not on *my* watch." Mother dropped the roaster on the floor at her feet. The larger cooker crashed into smaller pans and identified the source of the cymbal explosions. She grabbed another pan, then scrubbed the clean pot with the dish brush as if it had food stuck inside.

"Did you think I wouldn't find out?" Mother threw the brush in the sink, whipped around, and pinned Dad with a hard stare.

"What are you talking about?" He stepped closer and kneed a cabinet door shut.

She moved and blocked him from shutting another. "Is that why you sent my son away?" She stabbed his chest with her finger.

"No one forced Travis to leave."

"Why couldn't you have waited to see if he's the baby's father? Now my son is at Franklin Overton's church, of all places. Got the call this evening. Mother Pat gave me an earful about my own son. *Our son*, Broddrick. Please tell me you knew nothing about this." Tears wet her face. "How can you let him go over there and play but not let him stay at his home church? Our musicians bicker and jockey for positions because they need a permanent leader. This confusion is disrupting New Hope, and the people are taking sides."

Dad reached for her hand. "He sinned even if he didn't father the child. He walked in the role of a husband without a God-given right to do so. There's a morality clause every staff member is required to adhere to. My children will not receive special treatment."

Mother snatched her hand away. "A letter of recommendation from the *former* pastor is required to play at another church in the fellowship. Did you forget I was raised under the bylaws?"

"Not everyone honors the by-laws if it means having a good musician, dear." Dad remained calm and stepped closer. He wrapped his arms around Mother. She dropped her head to his chest and wept as he stroked her back. "He's grown and knows the truth. We can only pray."

She lifted her head. "Did you see your youngest daughter leaving here tonight? I hear tales of her visiting those party rooms." Mother turned her gaze toward Sharonda who remained in the doorway. "She's at one of those clubs, isn't she?"

Sharonda darted her eyes to the chaos around them.

"You don't know that. And it's a Thursday night." Dad cupped Mother's face.

Girl's night. Free drinks. And admission. Not that Sharonda had ever gone, but Janice and whomever she'd been on the phone with were looking to take advantage of the perks.

Mother pushed against Dad's chest.

He all but tripped over the scattered cookware on the floor.

Mother folded her arms. "That get-up Janice had on was so short she could've been one of Tina Turner's back-up girl's shaking a tail feather. Praying is good, but you *need* to say something to her."

"Go rest, Marianne. I'll finish the dishes." He nudged her from the sink and stuck his hands in the soapy water. "Lord, Jesus!" Dad sucked air between his teeth. "That's hot."

"Don't take the Lord's name in vain. We've already got two strikes."

He flung soap and water. "God does not keep account of our wrongs."

Mother snagged the dish cloth from the oven handle and made a homemade icepack. She returned to Dad and wrapped his fingers. Gently. As if caring came without thought. "Sometimes, I feel like Satan's winning."

"Lies. The enemy is already defeated." He gathered his wife into his arms again and she appeared to wilt into his embrace.

"Sharonda, can you take care of things while I see your mother off to bed?"

Moments like these drove Sharonda to find a way to help her family—at any cost. "Sure, Dad. Oh, I forgot to mention, I'm meeting Brice tonight at The Barrel."

Mother raised her head. "Oh, that's good. Make sure to look your best. Eat before you go. You wouldn't want to be hungry. Men like their women—"

"Have a good time. Let Brice know we asked about him." Dad pressed his wife's head to his chest and stroked her back.

Sharonda unclenched her jaw. Leave it to Dad to play mediator. "I will. Everything is going to work out, Mother."

"Remember to have that talk. Marrying sooner will help your situation *and* the church. Just think, if Dad is elevated to the Suffragan bishop vacancy, one level below the Bishop, Brice will be happy when he moves into the pastor position so quickly. Since he's a musician, he can take over the minister of music duties." Mother smiled at Dad. "It's possible I've overreacted. God could be using our daughter to defeat that enemy for sure. Let's go to bed, honey." They walked past Sharonda and headed toward their bedroom.

Hold your tongue. Why fight when everyone was getting what they wanted?

Sharonda perused the candies and whatnots for sale in The Barrel's general store. As soon as she picked up a wooden replica of a John Deer tractor, someone wrapped his arms around her waist from behind. She fumbled her grip on the toy.

"Aww, don't be skittish." Brice pecked her cheek. "Although your innocence is one of the things I like best about you."

Sharonda spun around, placing the tractor between them. "You scared me." Was she wrong for not volunteering her past?

"Are you thinking what I'm thinking? A boy first?" His dark eyes probed. "I'm glad you're finally ready to solidify a date. To think I proposed a year ago."

"I thought it a verbal agreement with my parents. You never presented me with a ring or popped the question."

He tapped the tractor. "Ah. My girl's feeling cheated. I'll have to rectify that. And soon. When I'm finished, you'll know who you belong to." He grinned, but unlike Carl Ray's, his gaze held a calculated coolness, a look that belonged to a lion positioned to pounce.

Why didn't this handsome specimen move her emotions? Tall, his smooth black skin accentuated his charcoal-gray and blue pinstripe suit in ways that attracted most women. Yet, nothing. No zing, pop, or anything.

Different women throughout the room appeared to ogle Brice. Then, their gaze landed on her. Some, bolder than others, frowned as if questioning what he was doing with the likes of her. She pulled at her nude blouse hanging loose over a pair of blue slacks. Standing next to him in his preacher finery, her more relaxed attire turned drab before her eyes.

"I see you got my message." She placed the toy back on the shelf.

"McDowel, party of five, your table is ready." The call punctuated over the intercom.

Five? A different family, perhaps? "Brice?" Sharonda searched his expression. He wouldn't have brought anyone along knowing she'd asked him here to discuss her medical issues and pick an earlier wedding date, would he?

He called over her head. "John, go get the table. Give me a minute."

Sharonda turned toward the person Brice addressed.

John stood taller than Brice, with a complexion light enough to expose freckles across the bridge of his nose. Closer to Sharonda's age, he was a suit and bow tie brother. He escorted a woman with blonde-tipped bangs and two older gentlemen—one bowlegged and the other sporting a full gray beard and a potbelly. "Who are they?"

Brice gripped her hand and squeezed. "Did you think I traveled alone? John is my newly appointed armor bearer. The others came to support my ministry. They offered their gifted voices tonight. After all they've done, the least I can do is feed them." As if he spoke to a simpleton, he drew his words out slower than crystalizing honey. His pasted smile did nothing to calm her rising frustration.

"I just thought—"

He placed his index finger on her lips.

Sharonda bristled at the roughness of his touch.

"You're not the jealous type, are you? Being a pastor's daughter, I didn't think I'd have to school you on what to expect."

She stepped back to break contact. "No, I understand. I assumed we'd discuss my concerns in private. Shouldn't we spend time together— the two of us—and get to know one another better? Especially if we are to marry sooner. With your traveling, we've spent so little time alone."

"I know all I need to know about you. We're both saved. My parents have been married fifty-three years. It's what makes their ministry strong. Mine will be strong too. You'll never have to worry about me cheating or divorcing you. We'll have sons and I'll raise them to take my place when the time comes. All you'll have to do is be a good wife. Support your man. And obey." He stroked her jawline and placed a soft peck at each corner of her mouth.

The kiss was gentle. Respectable. "Are we going to get a second table? I don't see how we can talk with an audience."

"There's no need for discussion. Your message said to see if an earlier date was possible for the wedding. The sooner the better. I'll make it happen."

Really? Then why couldn't he come up with any time to visit her. If it wasn't a revival, he claimed too many church responsibilities. Sharonda shook her head and stepped back into someone.

"Sorry, ma'am." Sharonda gazed up at the youth. By the looks of him, he'd rival Shaquille O'Neal when he finished growing.

"It was my—"

Brice grabbed the boy's arms and pinned them to his side. "Next time, watch where you're going."

His eyes widened.

"Brice! Let him go. You're scaring him." Sharonda smacked Brice's hand away.

"I didn't hurt him. Just teaching him a lesson." He reached out as if to tap the youth on the shoulder.

The young man recoiled and glanced several times at Sharonda. "I'm really sorry. It was an accident." He hurried off.

Brice laughed. "I can't wait to raise *my* boys."

Sharonda placed a protective hand over her abdomen. Was this the kind of man she wanted fathering her children? What if she only had one? And if a girl … had she not made her situation clear to Brice? He wanted *sons*.

"Come on, now. You're not mad at me, are you? The boy is fine, just a little soft."

She tugged on the strap of her purse. "And you know all this in one look?"

"That's what's wrong with these young bucks, nowadays. Mama's boys. Not enough men training them up to be real black men."

"A little extreme, don't you think?"

He shrugged. "He'll be careful to look where he's going from now on. Now, let's go eat." Brice draped an arm over her shoulder. His sweet cologne soured her stomach.

She shrugged away from him. "I'm not hungry. You go on. Your *entourage* is waiting."

Brice tilted his head and challenged her with a stare.

She lifted her chin and refused to blink.

He grunted. "Send me the new date to update my calendar. I'll be in touch with your dad. Sorry about the unexpected company."

She nodded.

Brice leaned toward her.

She turned her head before he could press his damp lips to hers.

Again, he laughed. "Soon, you'll beg for my kisses."

Chapter Eight

Sunday evening, after a parents' planning session for the Youth Rally, Sharonda dashed down the hallway. "Excuse me, Mr. and Mrs. Dower?" she called to an elderly couple who strolled toward the exit. "May I speak with you, please?"

The man and his wife slowed, turned, and blessed her with genuine smiles.

"Good evening, Sister Peterson." Mr. Dower held his wife's hand. "How can we help you?"

Sharonda closed the distance. "I want you to know that I see what you're doing for Patience." She faltered at the moisture building in Mrs. Dower's eyes. "I believe your youngest is in her thirties. It couldn't be easy starting over with a teenager."

Mrs. Dower nodded. Her husband handed her his handkerchief, and she dabbed the corners of her eyes. "I don't think we're doing a good job. Patience is more withdrawn now than she was when she came to live with us two years ago."

Her husband pulled her to his side.

"That's what I wanted to speak to you about. There's a support organization—We Grow Up—for the children of domestic violence. They have a booth at the annual youth event. Their founder, Ms. Greene, gives insight into a child's struggles after losing a parent. Would this be something you'd be willing to research and see if the program might be a benefit?"

The couple nodded.

61

"I have the foundation's pamphlets with information on their blog, support groups, and outreach services." Sharonda clasped her hands together. "Patience is special. I'd hate to see you give up on her."

Mrs. Dower hid her face against her husband's chest.

"I'm sorry if I've overstepped boundaries. I didn't mean to make matters worse."

Mr. Dower wrapped his arms around his wife. "No. Thank you for caring. We appreciate your kindness. Don't we, Alma?"

She sniffed. "We thought we were helping when we moved her to the opposite end of Texas, but she rejects everything we try to do. Here lately, I wondered if she'd been better off living with some of her father's relatives."

Sharonda shifted her weight from one foot to the other. "If you don't mind me asking, how did she come to live with you?"

Mr. Dower looked down at his wife.

She nodded once as if giving him permission to speak.

"We were neighbors. When the child's mother was killed, she ran to our house. Over the course of time, no family members claimed responsibility, so we went through the process and received the rights to care for her," he said.

Alma patted his chest, then faced Sharonda. "Patience's father is in prison for life for killing her mother. We couldn't see leaving her behind when we moved here."

"If you feel you've done all you can do, why did you come out tonight?"

Alma's face lit. "I watch the way Patience responds to you. Whatever you're doing reaches her. I guess we wanted to learn what you're saying so we can do the same at home. She brags that you give the best hugs."

Sharonda put her hands on her hips and sassed in a playful manner. "So, my extra fluff is good for something."

Mr. Dower chuckled. "I wish my heart was as big as yours, young lady. Right, sweetheart?" He squeezed his wife's shoulder.

She reached out and clasped Sharonda's hand. "Anything you need us to do to make your event a success, just say the word. We came to the meeting tonight as a last hope. The fact that you came to us is sign enough for us to keep trying. I'd love to get more information on the organization you mentioned."

A big heart. Here she'd come to be a help to them, and they'd affirmed her, seeing past the outer layers. She fidgeted under their praise. Every parent could learn from their example.

The corners of Sharonda's eyes stung. "The fact you care is what's important. I'll gather the We Grow Up information packets I have and get them to you."

"We appreciate you. Can we have one of your famous hugs?" Mrs. Dower lifted her arm, inviting Sharonda into an embrace of three.

Tears splashed Sharonda's cheeks. Unlike her parents, their affectionate ways replenished her empty reservoir.

⁓

When Carl entered the Youth Building, he heard Sharonda speaking to someone, but he didn't see her. He moved through the hallways, following the sound of her voice. When had an apology become so taboo? The frustrating woman had avoided him since the play two weeks ago. Yet Sharonda had crowded his thoughts since then, where new song ideas once thrived. Carl peeked around the next corner.

Sharonda's full attention zeroed in on the people near the exit. He slid behind a classroom door left ajar and within hearing.

Sharonda encouraged the couple.

Hopefully, this kid, Patience, understood what it meant to have Sharonda in her corner. Carl touched his face. He'd been the skinny guy in high school with blistering acne spotting his light-brown complexion a bright red. Then she'd invited him to church and introduced him to her older brother Travis, telling him how good Carl could sing and play piano.

Forever changing my life.

"So, my extra fluff is good for something." Sharonda's voice broke into his thoughts. She ran both hands over her denim skirt, much like he'd witnessed her doing the night of the play.

Carl had to bite down to keep from speaking out, considering he'd always been drawn to everything about her.

"I wish my heart was as big as yours," the man said.

Sharonda championed everyone she loved. Who defended her?

He ached to join them, to hold Sharonda close, and encourage her. Instead, Carl waited for the group to grow silent. He peered around the door to witness the couple exit the building.

Sharonda rocked from side to side with her arms wrapped across her chest.

When she walked in his direction, he stepped from behind the door. "Can I have a hug too?" He extended his arms.

❧

Sharonda jumped. *If you looked up when you walk...* Janice's reprimand surfaced. She stepped into Carl Ray's embrace. "Did you hear them? They said I convinced them not to give up on Patience."

"I heard." He stroked her hair.

"She's only acting out because the kids pick on her. Patience towers over both girls and boys right now. You ought to see her, Carl Ray. She's so beautiful. So much potential. In time, she'll grow into her long arms and big feet."

"Is that how you saw me when you championed me to your brother? What I was going to be, given time?"

She tilted her head back to look into his face. "You were so shy, but in choir, you came alive. Anytime you sang or played the piano everyone stopped and paid attention." She smiled with the memories.

Footsteps rang, cutting her musings short.

"Hide." Sharonda pulled Carl Ray inside the empty classroom. "I didn't mean to blubber all over your clothes. What are you doing here?" She spoke low.

"Coming to find you."

The Apology. "Not again." Sharonda attempted to move away but he caught her by the waist and pulled her back to his chest.

Carl Ray pressed his cheek against hers and whispered. "You've got to be still, or they'll hear you."

Voices grew louder.

Her heart raced.

"Deacon Ross, can you get the television on in this room?" From somewhere down the hallway, Mother's request could be heard over the other voices.

"Oh, no." Sharonda tried to pull away, but Carl Ray held firm and gently pushed her mouth against his shoulder, smothering her ability to speak.

"Shhh. A moment ago, you rushed into my arms." He chuckled.

Sharonda squirmed, but he didn't let her go.

He dropped his hand from the back of her head.

She whispered, "There's nothing funny about Mother finding *us* here."

"They'll most likely go into the first classroom. This is the second. Now, relax and let me hold you for a while longer. I have a few things to say."

She tensed.

Muffled voices filled the adjacent room.

"Relax. The apology can wait. This is more important." Carl Ray stroked her hair. "You *are* a beautiful woman." He ran his hand down her back. "All of you."

She encircled his waist and relaxed her full weight against him. In his arms, she could believe anything.

"Hey, sounds like they are preoccupied with whatever they're watching. We should be able to leave without anyone noticing."

Carl Ray released her so quickly, Sharonda stumbled.

"Let's go." He held her elbow.

She jerked her arm out of his reach. "You go. I'll follow in a bit." Again, she'd let her guard down.

"Sharonda?"

"Go."

His tall silhouette filled the doorframe as he looked up and down the hall, then turned toward the exit the Dowers had used. Always leaving.

Her shoulders lowered at the soft click from the door down the hall. She slumped onto the stool near the whiteboard. Another incident like this, and she might forget her arrangement with Brice.

Chapter Nine

The clock in Carl Ray's truck displayed six fifty-five. The church secretary had informed him of an emergency meeting at seven that Monday evening. He hurried into the conference room adjoined to Pastor Peterson's second residence away from home. If Carl remembered correctly, Pastor's and First Lady's offices were equipped with a personal bathroom and full-sized showers, closets stocked with ceremonial robes, and church clothing for the days they couldn't return home between services.

Seated at the long table were board members, assistant pastors, and other department leaders. They chatted in groups of twos and threes. Extra seats sat against the walls. Zeroing in on the back corner, he skirted behind several people to get to the empty chair. He sat without looking up.

The smell of warm vanilla and berries floated on the air. Carl stifled a moan and looked to his right. Not that he needed another dose of the intoxicating fragrance—one that had seeped into his dreams, chasing away sleep with vivid images of Sharonda in his arms. He pressed a finger against the throb at his temple.

Next to him, Sharonda sat poised with her pen and paper ready. She held her head high, her thick mane tucked into a clip, and she angled away from him.

Good, ignore me. Sitting next to her was distraction enough and he needed to focus. Carl turned to his left and extended his hand to Brother Daniels. The man accepted his greeting.

"I haven't had the chance to welcome you aboard. Just returned from a mission trip with the Smiths in Jamaica. But after I settle in, we'll have to have lunch and catch up," Daniels said.

"Sounds great." Carl leaned toward Sharonda. "Hello."

She spared him a quick nod.

Why the silent treatment? Had she guessed his reasons for leaving the classroom in such a hurry yesterday? What started out as a pure attempt to comfort turned into so much more. When she'd come back into his arms the second time, he wanted to give in to desires to champion her. She trusted him when he didn't trust himself. He felt it in the way her body relaxed against his. In that moment, his heart surrendered to her cause without consulting him. The suddenness had him floundering.

He pulled at his collared shirt as he remembered Sharonda scrambling to keep her balance and his clumsy escape.

Brother Daniels waved a stack of papers in front of his face.

"Sorry, my mind was somewhere else." Carl took one and passed the stack to Sharonda.

When his hands brushed hers, their gazes met. His presence *did* affect her. Did some of her wariness have anything to do with the connection they'd experienced last night? Carl Ray bowed his head as Pastor Peterson stood and opened the meeting with prayer.

Pastor sighed. "Did you see the latest Facebook phenomenon on the news Sunday evening? I've been on calls throughout the day with our organization's leader, Diocesan Bishop Charles Mitchell. He asked me why New Hope has not been more of a voice for God in the recent racial uproar. I couldn't give him an answer." Pastor scanned the room. "Here it is, a little brick church, right on Main Street in Lindale, Texas, has Interstate 20 blocked with cars, all because people wanted to hug the preacher's neck. Seven days he's been toting signs declaring 'All Lives Matter.'"

He paced back and forth. "It's not a competition, but it fills my heart with shame that we have triple their resources, yet they find a way to show love. The man is out there, only drinks water during the hottest part of the day, and leaves after night falls. Do you know who is supplying the water?"

68

When no one answered, he struck the table. "The people. Saved. Unsaved. Black. White. Hispanic. Women. Men. Law Enforcement. The fire department … that's true revival. When the truth sets the captives free, all people are drawn together in love. Maybe we've gotten too big and forgotten what really matters." He raked a hand over his salt-and-pepper hair. "That's the kind of church I was raised in. I'm convicted, saints." The stout man covered his face and dropped into his chair at the head of the table. "The truth is, people still care. This little country church leader took the time to show the world love is still alive. Look what *one* can do. Just think if we came together, lending our resources, how many people we could touch."

Silence pervaded the room.

Carl cleared the emotion from the back of his throat. In the presence of such raw passion, he longed to champion something bigger than himself. He pivoted enough to keep Sharonda within his periphery. What if God's plan included the woman who sat next to him? Working side by side in ministry. Who could stop them? A partner for life. He craved it. Could that partnership smell of vanilla and berries? "Hmm."

Sharonda whispered, "Are you okay?"

Carl gave a quick nod and sat straighter.

First Lady Peterson stood and walked to her husband. "Now that you've had time to reflect on the man of God's heartfelt concerns, I urge you to create a plan of action." She laid a dainty hand on her husband's shoulder.

As if Pastor drew strength from her nearness, the lines smoothed from his brow and he smiled.

Lady Peterson's piercing gaze traveled the room. "Our diocesan bishop desires to play a role in eradicating the racial tension sweeping the nation. This also happens to be the year he is searching for an assistant to fill the new Suffragan bishop vacancy made by the passing of the late Bishop Turner. Don't you see the opportunity for your leader? We give the diocesan what he wants, and he'll automatically look to Pastor Peterson."

Several board members raised their hands.

"Yes." First Lady Peterson acknowledged a man seated at the table.

"Do we really want to get named among such political matters? There's so much unrest with the Trump administration taking over after Obama."

Lady Peterson stood as straight as her petite frame would allow. "Did you hear my husband just now, Mr. Newsome? When did love become a political issue? If I remember right, Jesus reached out to the harlot as well as the tax collector, the Jew as well as the Gentile."

Pastor placed his hand over hers on his shoulder and squeezed.

She peered down into his smiling face.

He rose. "I value the insight of my leaders. As my beautiful wife has pointed out, I spoke my feelings. I hope you embrace my vision and come up with some ideas as to our plan of action. I hadn't considered the upcoming nomination for Suffragan bishop, but my wife's ever perceptive eye for details continues to bless this ministry. And me." He gave her a tender look. "Thank you for always having my best interest at heart and believing in me, dear."

Pastor again faced the group assembled. "However, no matter the Suffragan Bishop nomination, I want to be a part of bringing harmony back into our country. I'm not a Republican or a Democrat, but a *Biblocrat* if I have to come up with a party to support. You'll find my allegiance with whatever the Bible says. Knowing this, come up with something we can do. Let's meet again Wednesday after Bible study for anyone who's not ready to share an idea. Until then, you're dismissed."

Carl lingered in the charged atmosphere. The room seemed to pulse to the beat of minds turning, racing to come up with an idea. If they were like him, it'd be hard to ignore the challenge. He yearned to have a piece of staff sheet on hand to pen the notes and rhythms playing out in his head. The passionate speech stimulated his creative juices.

"What is it?" Sharonda stood at his side, her hand on his shoulder. Her touch mimicked her mother's support for her father.

The contact heightened the high of the moment. He looked up, hoping she glimpsed his heart's desire for them to be such a team. For her to be his soul mate. Oh, the things he could do with a wife at his side, embracing his own vision. "Music. I hear it. In here," he tapped his temple. "And here," he tapped his chest.

Sharonda removed her hand so quickly Carl wondered if his words offended her.

"When do you plan to go back on the road?" She hugged the legal pad close to her chest and looked away.

Carl stood but kept his voice low. "Hey, look at me."

Stragglers spoke to the pastor on their way out.

Sharonda hiked her chin before meeting his gaze.

"Why the sadness? Does the potential of my leaving bother you?" He studied her expression.

"Your talent reaches beyond any walls. It was never meant to be contained. New Hope is simply a resting place for you."

He went to touch her arm.

Sharonda stepped out of his reach and shot a quick glance at her mother.

She stood near the door watching them.

Carl offered Lady Peterson a smile.

"You didn't answer my question." He recaptured Sharonda's gaze.

"My feelings are irrelevant."

He searched the depths of her eyes for any fight she might have for him. "Not to me."

A flicker.

Carl gave her his best smile. He didn't care who witnessed their interaction.

Lady Peterson called out, "We're ready to go." She waved her daughter forward.

"Yes, Mother." Sharonda moved toward the door, paused, and looked over her shoulder. With her eyes not quite reaching his, she smiled. "Thank you."

"Carl, you need to get with Pastor. Complaints about your band members are crossing our desk. While the ladies sing your praises, your fellow band mates don't seem to embrace the same thinking. Good looks and talent only take you so far. Leadership is a honed skill." Lady Peterson spoke loud enough for everyone in the room to hear.

He focused on the first lady as she gave her evaluation. The truth acted like salt to an open wound. He had failed to reach the men entrusted to his leadership.

Sharonda stared her mother down.

"Yes, ma'am, I'm aware of the current situation. I have some things I'm working on. As soon as I know my next move, I'll be sure to book an appointment with Pastor Peterson." An urge to sweep Sharonda up in his arms and kiss her breathless swept through Carl. In time, he'd pursue the possibilities.

"Sounds good, Carl." Pastor wrapped his arm around his wife's waist and waved his hand for Sharonda to precede them, ushering his family from the room.

If this setting-his-house-in-order business included getting the girl, the task just got harder. What father in the ministry wanted a failure for a son-in-law? Carl left the church, weighed down with indecision.

What could he say that he hadn't already said to the band? What about his career? He didn't dare declare his feelings for Sharonda to Pastor with so much hanging over his head.

✍

Sharonda entered the house after the emergency meeting and walked past her sister without speaking. She longed to be in her bedroom alone with her thoughts.

"Where are you going?" Janice pulled a pan from the oven. "Hope you're hungry. I made your favorites."

Sharonda slowed, took a deep inhale. "Roast and potatoes?"

"Slow cooked in its own gravy. The way you like it." Janice shrugged, a silly grin on her lips.

"Maybe later."

"Any later and it'll be dry," Janice whined. "Most families have eaten by now. Only *this* one had an emergency meeting at seven *in the evening*."

"Got to wait for people to get off work and feed their kiddos. You know the routine." Sharonda softened her words and gave her sister a side hug. "A pastor's life is one of sacrifice and it extends to his family."

"That's why I'm going to get me a man *outside* the church. No meetings, services, or hospital trips." Janice huffed.

"You say that now." Sharonda released her and headed for the door.

"Hold up, missy." Mother entered the kitchen from the garage.

Although Sharonda shortened her steps, she kept walking.

"Sharonda Lorraine Peterson."

She stopped and turned around. "Ma'am?"

"Does this rash of insolence have anything to do with the way you were throwing yourself at Carl today?"

"Mother—"

"I mean, really." Mother flung her notepad on the table. "You looked desperate for attention. Grinning and going on like some school girl. Save it for Brice. You are the *oldest* daughter and I've groomed you to marry a pastor. I love Carl, but we preacher's kids have a different call on our lives."

Sharonda fisted her hands on her hips. "Wasn't it you at the dinner table trying to pair Carl Ray with Janice when he'd first returned? She's a PK."

"This is *not* about Janice. I'm talking to *you*."

"Maybe you should've spent more time giving Travis the marriage talk before he went out doing what it takes to make a baby." Sharonda raised her voice.

"Don't sass me, girl." Mother closed the space, inches from Sharonda. "Singing together and marrying is *not* the same thing." She glared up at her.

"What's going on in here?" Dad walked in from the garage, pushing his cell phone into his jacket pocket.

"Nothing you need to worry about." Mother went to him and softened her words as if she'd never been upset. "How did your call with the Diocesan go?"

73

"Can a man eat before he's interrogated?"

"You're right. After dinner." Mother smiled at Janice. "Everything smells great."

Sharonda bristled inside. Mother's pretending everything was okay left a bad taste in her mouth. She lifted pleading eyes to her father. "I was headed to my room if you don't need me for anything."

"Go on, baby." Dad said.

"He *needs* you to honor the arrangements he's made with Brice on your behalf." Mother knew how to dig in her claws.

Chapter Ten

Locked in her bedroom, Sharonda kicked her shoes off and peeled out of the binding girdle. Her phone buzzed. Brice's charming features appeared over the face of her Galaxy. She let the call go to voicemail and collapsed onto her bed.

My feelings are irrelevant.

She mouthed Carl Ray's words. *Not to me. Not to me. Not to me.* His response had dropped from his lips, echoing against the deep well of her soul.

Did he really care? "Carl Ray, why toy with my emotions?" Sharonda moaned and rolled over on her back. "Soon, you'll return to New York. I can be strong a little while longer." A tear slipped from the corner of her eye. "Oh, God, I know I promised to be good but ..." Another one fell. She flipped on her side and buried her face in the comforter.

The door rattled. "Sharonda."

She tensed, held her breath, and wished Janice away.

"Don't make me call Mom. Open. The. Door."

Sharonda screamed into her pillow.

Another shake of the knob caused Sharonda to sit up.

"I'm not going away."

Sharonda stomped to the door and unlocked it but refused to play lady doorman. Leaving her sister to stand outside, she walked to the closet and disrobed.

The knob rattled again.

Sharonda's hands stilled on the wooden hanger as she waited for her sister to announce her entrance with some lame wisecrack.

Blessed silence.

She secured her suit jacket on a hanger. After storing her skirt and blouse, Sharonda continued to face the diminishing number of outfits she could still squeeze into. So what if she stood in her big cotton unmentionables? Maybe Janice would take the hint to go somewhere else.

Janice tapped her shoulder. *Or not.*

"I hate you," Sharonda said without turning.

Baby girl rested her head on Sharonda's back. "Tell me something I don't already know. This love-hate relationship of ours has to stop. Tell me what I did," she pleaded. "I want my big sister back."

Sharonda turned and gathered Janice in her arms. "It's not you. I'm just an old biddy." She sighed.

"You don't have to be. Carl Ray came home."

"I didn't say an old *maid*." Sharonda broke their embrace to wipe her cheeks. "He came home for health reasons, *not* to see me. Get a good look at me, dear. You know how many times I've tried to change, but I'm stuck in this body." Sharonda sniffed. "As of today"—she pointed to the girdle draped over the basket in her closet—"I refuse to hide the real me underneath all those contraptions. Not even for him." She stepped past Janice and went to the dresser for sweats and a T-shirt. "Wasn't it you who told me to stop pretending?"

"Then you're going after him? Mom can't dictate who you"—Janice made air quotes—"throw yourself at?" She giggled.

"You don't listen. I'm not his type."

"He wanted *your type* to have that golden ticket. His face glowed as if someone offered him a plate of warm chocolate chip cookies with a glass of milk." Janice winked. "You can be the caramel drizzled on top."

Sharonda jerked the shirt over her head and punched her arms through the sleeves. "Don't tempt me when I'm weak. A second time around with Carl Ray, and I may not come out so lucky. Then there's the fact you like to ignore. I'm marrying Brice. Mother's orders." She saluted.

"Seriously, though. Another scandal and who would nominate Dad as Suffragan bishop?"

Janice scrunched her nose. "What does Dad's nomination have to do with you marrying Carl Ray?"

Sharonda sighed. "There's this thing between us. When our lives aren't going well, we look to each other." She yanked the sweats up over her hips. "Our relationship is complicated. I'm a fallback girl to him, not the kind he'd stick around and commit to. I gave him the best of me. He didn't hesitate to leave town when his opportunity for fame came." She pressed her lips together and swallowed. "If you haven't done *it* already, don't."

Janice averted her eyes. "I know what everyone thinks of me, but I haven't gone that far. Don't get me wrong. I love me some kissing, but there's no one I want to share my life with. Dancing will have to do. Men these days! As soon as they discover I'm not puttin' out, they take off. I really believe Carl is back because he wants to do things right this time around."

"Right for who?"

Janice shrugged. "I guess that's what you'll have to find out."

She folded her arms. "Did you know, I've managed to avoid him every time he tries to utter his unsolicited regrets?"

Janice sat cross-legged on her bed and motioned for Sharonda to join her.

"Carl Ray is too big for this town. It would be a waste to have him committing his life to me based on some moral code he's bought into. I do have *some* pride." She flopped on her own bed. "No one, no matter how desperate, wants to be someone's charity case."

"Why can't he be in love with you and regret walking away from the best thing that ever happened to him?"

"Make-believe. You watch too many movies." Sharonda sat up and threw a pillow at her sister.

"You're beautiful." Janice paused as if admiring a work of art. "Why wouldn't he want more? He's a Christian now. He wouldn't lie about his feelings for you."

"Wait. *Now*, you're trusting us so-called Christians?"

"Carl has stood by his word, unlike the people in this family." Janice smirked and launched the pillow back at Sharonda.

"Who knew Carl Ray's arrival would inspire a change in you? Call me a coward. If I anticipate more and he leaves again …" She leaned against her headboard. "You heard Mother. It's my duty as the firstborn daughter to marry a pastor. Speaking of …" Sharonda retrieved her phone from her dresser. "I need to return Brice's call. We have a wedding to plan. Did I tell you we're moving the date up?"

"When?"

"As soon as I call him with the time and place. Brice is ready for sons." She tapped the phone against her chin. Why did she procrastinate?

"And that makes him a dirty old man. He may not look it, but subtract a few years, and you could've been his daughter. Better yet, you find the Bible verse where the oldest girl of a pastor is to marry one, and I'll sing at your wedding."

"You are so crazy." Sharonda laughed, and Janice joined in. "You must admit. Brice is so pretty, no one would guess the age difference."

Janice huffed. "Promise me you'll think about what I've said. In the meantime, come eat." She moved toward the door.

"I'm not hungry. Maybe later. You can leave a plate in the microwave for me."

"Love is known to steal the appetite."

Sharonda grabbed some bundled socks from the floor and hurled them at her sister's head. "Leave already."

Janice ducked. "Tell me you love me." She worked her neck like a dancing Cobra.

"More than words can convey. Love you, Peanut." Sharonda smiled.

"Aww. That wasn't so hard. Now that you've reminded your lips how to say the words, tell Carl." Janice cackled.

"Get out." She thrust her index finger toward the door. How could such a stunning girl have such an irritating laugh?

Sharonda grabbed her Bible and sat in her reading nook. She couldn't remember the last time she'd voluntarily read the Word outside of a church service. She thumbed through the pages to the book of Samuel. She hungered to hear about some other imperfect person besides herself. She'd grown up hearing about David, so the story played in her head like a movie even when the events recorded on the pages bounced across time periods without warning.

Hadn't the Bible referred to him as a man after God's heart? Was it his fault Bathsheba chose the wrong place to bathe? David did what any man would do, he got caught up. So what?

Sharonda grabbed several pages and flipped to a section labeled, "Nathan's Parable and David's Confession."

And if that had been too little, I also would have given you much more!

She skipped several paragraphs and read on.

For you did it secretly …

She blinked, and the next paragraph seemed to lift off the page.

I have sinned against the Lord.

Sharonda jumped up, threw the leather-bound book onto the chair, and fled the room. She hadn't eaten. That must be the reason her body shook.

The clock chimed ten as she reached for the plate Janice had stored in the microwave. She tucked herself in at the table and slid her glass of sweet tea closer. She forked a chunk of roast beef dripping in gravy. Every bite quieted the unrest in her thoughts.

Her situation differed from David's. He had a man killed. No one died because she and Carl Ray comforted each other. Things happened.

Sharonda leaned back and groaned. She'd polished off garlic mashed potatoes and several rolls with her large portion of roast. The heaviness in her chest returned as she shoved the plate away. She took her dinnerware to the dishwasher.

"Couldn't sleep?" Her dad came to stand next to her at the sink. "Are you okay?"

"Yeah." She loaded her dishes on the bottom rack. "Got caught up doing some reading."

"Intriguing enough to make you skip dinner?"

79

Sharonda held her breath and counted. She'd believe her dad wasn't making fun of her since they'd shared a type of truce since their falling out. "I happened to be reading my Bible."

"Oh?"

She squeezed the green gel into the soap dispenser before closing the door. "Dad, I've been thinking. We better prepare for Carl Ray's leaving."

"Do you know something I don't?"

There was the friction between Carl Ray and Aaron at the play, so she wasn't lying. "I overheard him and another musician having words. Mother mentioned at the meeting there're complaints. I'm thinking of you when I say you may want to reach out to Travis before Carl Ray abandons us for better opportunities. I believe those were your words?"

"Your brother went too far."

"Everybody makes mistakes. But let's think about the whole church. Maybe put the issue up for a vote. You can persuade the board to accept Travis again."

"Why are you suddenly a Travis supporter? What about Carl Ray? Does this have anything to do with you and Brice setting a date?"

"No." She fingered the bottom of her shirt. "Carl Ray is on the mend. You should've seen the crowd's response at the play. They'll have him back on the road, and we'll be stuck without a minister of music before I can marry Brice. And you know Mother can't stand change." Sharonda intended for her words to motivate her father, but she hadn't expected the flash of pain in his eyes.

"It's late." He patted her back. "Pray for your mother. Let's get some sleep. Tomorrow will come sooner than we think." His voice had taken on a weary quality to match the worry lines across his brow. "For the record, Brice is not the answer to your mother's problems or the church's. God is."

Dad had never openly expressed an opposing view to anything Mother voiced. Not that Sharonda could remember. "Yes, sir." She ducked her head. She hadn't intended to heap more stress on his shoulders. Once Carl Ray left town, she might not enjoy her humdrum life as much, but her days would be back to normal. Normal, she understood. Average, she would accept.

Dad moved to the light switch. "You go on. I'll lock up."

She approached and kissed his cheek. "Good night."

The lines on his face softened.

Sharonda had a call to make. Maybe if she and Brice met up one more time she could discover something about him that would calm her own fears about their future together.

～

"Hey, thanks for meeting with me so late." Carl shook Derrick's hand, brought it in for a quick chest bump, and patted his arm.

Derrick took the barstool next to Carl. "You order hot wings for me?"

"It's the least I can do since I asked you to meet. You could've said no."

"Anything to help the church. And I'm always hungry before a late-night set."

Carl lifted a brow. "Only establishment open this late besides food joints is the club."

"Drummers are at the bottom of the totem pole when it comes to church paper. Bills got to be paid."

Although some of what he said rang true, Derrick's decision to work the nighttime industry didn't set well with Carl. "How does the lifestyle surrounding club life affect your walk with Christ?"

"I won't lie. I've stepped out a time or two with some of the ladies. I've never done drugs. Mama being a crackhead motivated the restraint. Her spending her years trying to get the next high left me to take care of my baby brother." Derrick grabbed the hand sanitizer on the bar and swabbed the gel over his hands. "Experienced too many cold and hungry nights. No temptation in that department." He nodded at the bartender. "I'll have a Dr Pepper."

"That goes on my tab, Jimmy."

"Whatever you say, Rockstar."

Carl shook his head at his old classmate.

Derrick dropped a wingette into his mouth and pulled the meat from the bones with one big tug and lip smack. "They hired me to play the drums. My *walk* wasn't a part of the requirements." He talked between chews.

No wonder they resented his intrusion. *They've had free rein—no rules, no expectations.* "Gotcha. So how do we get this band back on track?"

"Aaron brought most of us on with him. There's history." Derrick wiped his fingers over a napkin. "What is it with you and this need for a Sunday class? If you gonna make us attend, at least make it interesting. I ain't the only one with a Saturday night hustle, and your lessons don't help to keep a brother alert."

"They're that bad?"

"Worse." Derrick chuckled. "The pastor's daughter creates the church's material. The way you two were eyeballing each other in the music room, I'm sure she'll be eager to help you."

"Sharonda avoids me." Carl dipped a carrot and celery sliver in ranch dressing. The carrot's sweetness made the green stuff bearable.

"Didn't y'all grow up together?"

"Time has a way of changing people."

Derrick waved his mini-drumstick at Carl. "Sounds like you got it bad."

"She knew me when nobody gave me a second look. Promoted me to her brother when I took my talent for granted. She was a real friend." Carl wished Derrick would go back to eating. Something about the guy made Carl say things best left unspoken.

"And you want more, don't you? I hear it in your voice."

"She's good to those kids at the church. Even the troubled ones. She defends them. They'll never have to worry if she'll stick around or not. And she's smart."

"Sounds more like you're looking for a mother for your future children." Derrick snickered behind his glass as he took a big gulp of soda. "You can have any woman out there. Why her?"

Carl slapped the bar. "Why *not* her?"

The bartender looked their way.

"Sorry," Carl said.

Derrick lifted both hands. "Whoa, I'm a friend not a foe."

Carl gripped the back of his neck. "Man, if I hear one more person make a sly remark about her ... She's perfect the way God made her." He closed his eyes and remembered her generous curves hugged against his body. *Lord, have mercy.*

"You know the saying: 'You like it. I love it for you.'" Derrick sucked the meat from another bone like a vacuum. "I like mine tall, dark, and timid. Give me a little mystery and I go bonkers for the hunt."

Carl tapped his abdomen where the skin puckered from his appendectomy. "Man, when you're flat on your back, struggling to live, you learn what really matters. I want somebody willing to fight by my side. That's Sharonda." He could still see her staring her mother down for his sake.

"By your smile, is it safe to say you're dating the pastor's daughter?"

"Not yet, but I plan to change that." Carl dropped the lemon wedge from the rim of the glass into his water, then drank.

"Good luck."

"I'd rather you pray. Some things are too important to leave to chance."

Derrick wiped his mouth. "You write some of that Romeo stuff into your lessons, and we may stay awake long enough to learn something."

"I'll work on getting us new material. Can I count on you to run intervention with the boys?"

"Sure. But you might want to focus on helping Aaron. I'd hate to see the guy lose his family. He's got three boys that need him. Like most of us, we ain't had a daddy to show us nothing. His wife is good people. In his own way, he loves her. He don't deserve her, but she loves him."

"How do you happen to know all of this?" Carl picked up a wingette.

Derrick licked the sauce off his thumbs and removed the rest with a napkin. "His wife is my sister."

"Would you eat it if you could see the sugar?" Brice dumped several packs of the white granules all over Sharonda's chocolate brownie.

She glanced around, dropped her napkin over her dessert, and hoped no one in the restaurant witnessed his actions. "Is this the treatment I am to expect as your wife?" Anger incinerated her initial embarrassment.

"You say that as if I've treated you wrong. Sugar Diabetes has claimed the lives of too many of my friends. I want the best for you. For us. Our children." He caressed her knuckles. "Forgive me, I didn't mean any harm."

Something in his tone made her want to understand him. *Relax. Voice your concerns and give him a chance to answer. Lord knows you're not perfect.* Sharonda released a death grip on her fork and returned it to the table.

Sugar Diabetes? She hadn't heard that term since the last time she'd visited her grandma. Only the older saints said it like that. He *is* older. "I'm not a kid to be bossed around and treated as if I can't think for myself."

Crow's feet imprinted between his brow and creases lined his mouth. He seemed confused. Maybe he really wasn't conscious of the way he came across.

"If anyone knows you're a woman, it's me." Rather than his usual self-assured pose, his words conveyed a genuine kindness. "I've been on my own too long. Thankfully, that will change soon. I can work at being more sensitive."

She liked this version of Brice better, but did the absence of his posse have anything to do with his change in attitude? She squeezed his hand before pulling hers free. "You have a large church following and people respect you. You're handsome and can have your choice of women. Why me?"

"I watch you. You serve your parents in a way that's not seen in the younger generation. I'm attracted to your maturity—one you'll need to serve at my side in ministry. And if I'm going to have sons, I'll need a

84

younger wife. Women my age either have children already, or they're not willing to try. Truth be told, I want children of my own loins." A boyish longing shone in his onyx eyes.

Loins? His age was *really* showing tonight. "What if we have a girl? What if we discover I'm not able to have children after all?"

He frowned. "Did the doctor predict problems?"

"Not exactly." She pushed the paper-covered brownie to the side. "She said sixty to seventy percent of women with my diagnosis are fertile. I just worry since they are recommending a hysterectomy." She couldn't bring herself to tell him they'd suggested she have the surgery this time next year. If they were blessed with one child, she'd suffer through another painful year for the chance at two.

"I'd love any children God saw fit to bless me with, boy or girl. I guess I've voiced my desire to have sons to carry on my name with too much emphasis."

"But could you live with me not being able to have children and possibly adopt?"

"Honestly, I don't know. If we'd talked earlier about your medical issues, I'd have had an opportunity to evaluate the situation. Now, I need time. Having my own is the reason—"

"You wanted to marry me. I understand. I'll wait for you to contact me with your decision."

Silence sat at their table like an uninvited guest. Where did they go from here? *Is my desire to give birth to my baby so wrong, God?*

Nothing.

What did she expect? She and God never agreed on anything. If they had, He would've made her skinny, Carl Ray would never have left, and her mother wouldn't be trashing their kitchen with pots and pans in the middle of the night.

Sharonda scooted her chair back. "Excuse me, I need to go to the ladies' room."

"Sure. Go." He stood, but she waved him to sit.

She grabbed her purse.

"Sharonda?"

"Carl Ray?"

He touched her arm. "I didn't expect to run into you here." His eyes locked on Brice. "This late."

Derrick walked up and grinned at Sharonda before addressing her guest.

"Reverend McDowel, it's been a long time. Good to see you." The drummer extended his hand.

Brice accepted his greeting, then stood. He squared his shoulders as if to put Carl Ray in his place.

Sharonda glanced at Carl Ray's hold on her arm. She moved away from his touch. "Brice, this is Carl Ray, our interim minister of music at New Hope. Carl Ray, Pastor Brice McDowel."

"Her fiancé," Brice added. He extended his hand to Sharonda.

She moved, taking her place at his side. He wrapped his arm around her back and displayed his awful wax smile.

Carl Ray blinked. "Congratulations. I didn't know."

"Nothing's official until we set a date," she stammered, her gaze on Carl Ray.

Brice stepped in front of her and blocked her view of Carl. "Is there something you need to tell me, Sharonda?"

Chapter Eleven

After an hour in her office, Sharonda tilted her head to stretch a kink from her neck and shoulder. Last night's debacle with Brice had left her tense.

"Looks like I came at the right time." Carl Ray paused in the doorway. "Can I come in?"

She froze. *No!*

"It's church business."

His demeanor reminded her of a young cowboy in a western asking his girl to the dance for the first time. Sharonda should've embraced this opportunity to distance herself, but her body wouldn't be controlled so easily. She nodded toward the two chairs in front of her desk. "Come on in."

He stood behind one of the wingbacks. "If you'll allow me, I can work out the tension. I've learned a lot from my masseuse."

"Please." *Remember, Carl Ray has to go.* Sharonda tilted her head left, then right.

"Let me close the door. Give you privacy."

"About last night—"

"Shhh." Carl wiggled his fingers. "First things first. No more than a couple minutes and you'll feel brand new. Kinked muscles don't stand a chance."

Nor my heart. "I'll be the judge."

"Do you have a clip?" He moved behind her chair.

She snagged the ponytail holder from inside her top drawer and secured the mass to the side.

His fingers slid down her neck. "You're in knots." He made small, medium, then large circles over her shoulders until he pressed in at a tender place near her blade.

Sharonda jerked away from his touch.

"Hold still. I have to apply pressure to get the muscle to relax."

She grimaced. "It hurts."

He bent close to her ear. "Trust me."

She blew out a long breath before she inhaled. His woodsy scent made rational reasoning almost impossible.

"Thata girl," Carl Ray said. He increased the pressure.

He hummed.

Sharonda dropped her jaw to cry out, but something released in her tight muscles. She stretched left and could extend farther.

"See, I told you."

She sighed. "Indeed, you did."

"Okay, take a breather, and I'll do the other side. Make sure you ice later and drink lots of water. You don't want to be too sore."

Sharonda repositioned her hair, and his hands went back to work. The muscles on the opposite side obeyed quicker as if he'd earned her body's trust. When he reached another tender spot, she embraced the pain, knowing the reward to come. Pressure. More pressure. Finally, muscles left cramped together too long relented.

Another deep inhale and exhale. "Thank you. I feel so much better."

He rested his hands on either side of her neck.

"Carl Ray—"

"Sharonda. Sorry." He stepped back. "I didn't mean to cut you off." He moved to open the door and returned to sit in the wingback chair.

She cleared her throat. "I really need to explain about last night."

He leaned forward. "Do you love him?"

How could she, when Carl Ray owned her heart? "So much has happened since you've been away."

"Don't get me wrong. It's a well-known fact that women are drawn to authority figures, and the preacher man has the *it* factor. The look, the confidence, and the church following, from what Derrick says, but I never would've known you were in a relationship if I hadn't run into you at the restaurant."

Sharonda fiddled with a paper clip on her desk. "You have every right to be confused. My arrangement with Brice is strange. A long story."

"I've got time." Carl Ray rested his ankle on top of the opposite knee. "Tell me why you're marrying a man you don't love."

Sharonda bent the clip. "Love is what you're willing to commit to, not some flighty emotion you read about in fairytales."

Carl Ray shrugged. "He's too old."

"Back in the day, women were given to men far older." She hurled the clip into the trash.

"Why do I sense your mother's involvement in this soap opera?" He crossed his arms.

"Brice's age is not the culprit. I need to marry." She sighed. "His age is a benefit to me. Unlike most indecisive younger men, he shares my need to start a family immediately."

"Now you sound like a rehearsed script. Surely someone is feeding you this nonsense. Why rush into a covenant relationship when you have plenty of time to have children. Preacher man could be eighty and still produce. But to be stuck with someone you don't love is too big a risk."

"The only one taking a chance in this situation is Brice. But now, he's having second thoughts." She bent another clip.

Carl Ray moved to the edge of his seat. "What am I missing?"

"Brice marries me and positions himself as the next pastor of New Hope. He wants sons to follow in his footsteps. If he gambles on my ability to have children, Dad hopefully gets promoted to Suffragan bishop. That will make Mother happy, thus healthier."

"And what's in the arrangement for you again? Brice isn't the only male on earth able to fertilize an egg."

"I need a hysterectomy," she blurted, tired of the back-and-forth.

His mouth opened, but thankfully, he didn't spout off some Christian rhetoric about accepting God's plans.

"Yeah, that's what I thought. He's the only one who wants me."

He shook his head. "You don't know that."

"In my experience, I'm not the type of woman men hang around for."

Carl Ray gripped the arms of the chair as if he would stand, then dropped his head.

"Forget I said anything." She waved him off.

"Sharonda—"

"*Thank you* for the massage." She picked up a red pen and circled the words Youth Event in the center of her desk calendar. She looked at Carl Ray. Would he consider a cameo?

She conjured a visual of her church kids as the choir, mixed in with a crowd of neighborhood children worshiping together. Carl Ray led the group with his silky tenor voice. Would he agree to help?

"Ask and you shall receive. But don't think this conversation is over." He laced his fingers, turned them inside out, and made his knuckles pop.

Goosebumps lifted the hairs on her arm. "I haven't even asked for your help." Had she missed something he'd said?

"You didn't have to. I offered. You would've done the same for me."

"We *do* work well together. If you're a part of the Youth Rally, it's sure to be a success and get the attention of our diocesan bishop. Who wouldn't want their assistant to be a man who shares their vision? My father is that man, Suffragan Bishop Broddrick Peterson. Sounds good, doesn't it?"

"What does that have to do with us?"

"Everything. The children are the future. What better cause to bring people together as one, putting their differences aside. If I'm going to pull this off, I *need* you." Hearing the words spoken out loud gave her a moment's pause. "What do you think about teaming up with me?"

"You read my mind."

"Great. Let's map out the details so we'll be ready to present our idea to Dad."

He frowned. "A presentation?"

"About you headlining at the annual Youth Rally. Your music has crossed over. Both KVNE and KJTX play your songs, filling households of every culture." She bounced on the edge of her seat. "Using your contacts, we can get a representative from most of the churches in Longview and give the world a picture of unity." She searched the blank look on his face. "What?"

﹏

Carl relocated to sit on the edge of her desk. "I've got to work on my communication skills with you."

She raised her brow. "I figured you'd want to work with the kids."

He laughed. "The very things I love about you also frustrate me. Why couldn't you be excited I wanted to work with *you*?"

She chewed her bottom lip.

"I believed you'd started to see us as a potential team, and you're finding ways to make your dad the next bishop."

She tapped her pen against the calendar.

Carl took the pen from her grasp and tucked it behind his ear. "What if I told you I don't care about your father becoming the next bishop? I care about *you*."

Sharonda looked away.

He rounded the desk and turned her chair to face him. "We can handle your health issues together. Let me love you the way you deserve. Build you up, not tear you down."

He bent and kissed the ridges on her forehead. "You don't have to settle. Preacher Man isn't the only one who wants you."

She looked at the door and tapped her fingers on the calendar.

He covered her hand. "Why do my words fluster you?"

"Don't get caught up in some kind of hero complex. Your life is in New York. Soon, you'll return to the stage. I'm forced to be a realist. My place is here. My family needs me." She tried to pull away, but he held firm.

"You take care of everyone else. Let me take care of *you*. What do you have to say about that?"

"Why?" she whispered.

"Because—"

"Hey, you two?" Derrick stood in the doorway. "Am I interrupting anything?"

"Yes." Carl Ray lifted Sharonda's fingers to his lips and kissed them. "Just so you know I'm serious." He smiled when her eyes widened, then faced the drummer. "Were you looking for me?"

Derrick's gaze appeared to shift to their clasped hands. "Yeah, but we can talk later. I see you took my advice." He winked at Sharonda. "Pastor is still bragging on your last published work. I told Carl to get you to help him write up some new Sunday material. Or else risk losing his entire band. Literally. He's killing us." Derrick chuckled. "Carl, come by the practice room when you're done." He smirked and left.

Carl turned to Sharonda.

Her eyes glistened.

"Hey, what's wrong?" He reached out.

Sharonda scooted her chair back and stood. "That's what all this is about? You needed a Sunday school curriculum?" She glanced at the ceiling, then back at him. "And for a moment I thought you actually …" She huffed and moved behind the chair.

Carl crossed his arms. "No. Say it."

She pressed her lips closed.

"Since you won't say it, I will. Cared about you? Yes, the 'extra fluff' and all. I happen to find you very attractive."

Sharonda batted her damp lashes and her bottom lip trembled.

The things this woman did to his heart. "I *did* come to ask you to help me with Sunday material for the band. I got distracted when I saw you in pain."

She shook her head. "You don't have to explain. I understand."

"No, I don't think you do. Until the day I overheard you talking to the couple in the hallway, I only thought to apologize. You defended Patience the same way you did me back in the day. Let *me* defend *you*." He stepped closer.

She didn't back away. That had to mean something.

"You saw my potential when I couldn't. I see *yours*. Tell me you don't feel the bond when we're together. Tell me I've imagined the connection, and I'll leave you alone." He took another step, nudging the chair aside. "I'm no longer a teenager, controlled simply by my emotions." Influenced, but not controlled.

She wrung her hands. "This feeling you're experiencing will go away when you get things right with the band. When you're completely healed and able to return to performing on the road full time. You won't even think of me. Don't you see? That's the connection you feel. It's temporary. When we're down, we come together and things are better for a moment."

Carl Ray pushed a strand of hair behind her ear. "I want more than a night. I'm not the same selfish kid. Let me prove it."

She stepped back. "This is what we'll do. Make a list of the topics you need to cover in your Sunday class. I'll compile information I already have, and we can arrange it into a workbook. In return, you help me with the Youth Rally. Once things are going well, if you still feel the same, maybe we can talk about us." Sharonda looked everywhere but at him.

Carl Ray smiled. "Do I need to contact Brice? Let him know not to waste his time? I'm prepared to do whatever it takes to make you believe me."

"Believe what?" First Lady Peterson waltzed into the room and laid a stack of files onto the corner of Sharonda's desk. "Carl, don't you have work to do? I believe we just had this discussion."

Sharonda moved away from him. "Guess what, Mother? Carl Ray and I will be working together on his band stuff, and in return, he's agreed to work with the youth for the rally. You'll get the details when we present them to Dad tomorrow."

Did she think he needed her to protect him? "And once the band issues are resolved, your daughter has agreed to let me pursue her until she believes me when I say I want to be more than friends," he added.

Sharonda mumbled, "Not quite."

Lady Peterson crossed her arms. "Hah! For how long? Carl Ray, your talents are too big for this place. Soon, you'll return to the life of the rich and famous. Sharonda has an offer on the table more suitable to her type. Right, dear?"

Carl Ray tried to capture her gaze. *Tell her you've changed your mind.*

Sharonda fidgeted with her dad-blasted shirt, her lips sealed.

"With all respect, First Lady Peterson, she will have to tell me that for herself. Until then, we have an arrangement." He approached Sharonda and lifted her chin. "I'll start calling in some favors. Every church and radio station in East Texas will want to help with the rally. Answer your phone when I call." He placed her pen back on the calendar.

"Okay." She glanced at her mother.

"First Lady Peterson? You have a good day." He left, having had the last word.

꧁

Sharonda stared after Carl Ray. He defended her against Mother. Sharonda laid a hand at the base of her throat.

"Don't be stupid." Mother stamped her foot. "When will you learn?"

"Learn what? I have my doctorate in theology. I do pretty much anything you tell me to do. What would you have me learn?" Sharonda lifted her chin.

Mother's gaze traveled up and down Sharonda. "I know you better than you know yourself."

No. You don't.

"You give in to Carl Ray, and you'll regret it for the rest of your life. I can smell the lust spewing from your pores." An incoming call interrupted Mother's monologue. She dug into her purse and extracted her smartphone. "Hello, Lena. I'm with my daughter. Can I call you back?" She grabbed the pen from the desk and jotted *Arabella 11:00 a.m.* on Sharonda's calendar. "Yes, ma'am. I will." Mother ended the call and threw the pen along with the phone into her purse. "We'll continue this conversation later, at home. I have to go."

94

Chapter Twelve

The bedroom door banged open.

Sharonda lifted her head from reading the New Testament chapter.

"There you are." Mother waltzed over to her bed. She looked like she'd stepped straight off the cover of a fashion magazine in her yellow blouse paired with crop-seersucker bottoms. "Put some clothes on and let's go."

Sharonda clamped her jaw so hard her molars pulsed under the pressure. She glanced down at her jeans and cotton V-neck.

"I didn't stutter." Mother tossed her Bible on the bed. "The sooner we go and come back, the sooner you can return to your reading."

"Where are we going?"

"The Arabella."

"Didn't you go yesterday after Lena's call? Is Grandma sick?" Sharonda trudged to the closet.

"Does she have to be ailing for us to visit? I hate to think what you girls will do when it's me in a senior living community. Will y'all leave the responsibility to strangers to care for me?"

Sharonda rifled through her clothes and called over her shoulder, "You're being dramatic."

"And *you* have developed a wicked tongue. Is it your time again?" She headed toward the bathroom.

"No, Mother, you're just not accustomed to hearing *my* thoughts. Maybe turning thirty loosened my tongue."

She halted and turned. "Since you know the reason for the problem, I'll expect you to fix it, young lady. Better yet, ask God to renew the right thinking."

After you. Sharonda yanked the black dress off the hanger. Too formal, but she'd appear thinner. Anything to avoid Grandma's vicious tongue as well. She moved past her mother into the bathroom.

"I'll be waiting in the car," her mother said from the other side of the closed door.

When Sharonda entered the SUV, she slumped in her seat, facing the window. Counting road signs and memorizing the expansive landscapes of the mansions tucked away in unsuspected wooded neighborhoods, she endured the trip through town without saying a word. She exhaled as Mother maneuvered the circle drive around the manicured fountain, past the cottages, and parked close to her grandmother's apartment entrance.

Standing outside the door, her mother pulled Sharonda's shoulders back. "You don't have to hunch over and tell everyone with eyes how big a burden it is to carry *those* things."

Breasts? They have a name. "Yes, ma'am."

"I expect you to be on your best behavior." Mother knocked.

Sharonda tapped her toe on the porch.

"Use your key, Marianne." Her grandma's voice exploded from the other side of the closed door.

Mother fumbled in her purse for the key. "Mom, we're in."

"Took you long enough. I'll be out in a few. Got to finish my show." Grandma spoke from her bedroom.

Mother walked the room while a daytime judge's intelligent sarcasm played in the background. She stopped in front of the Sterling Silver wedding frames of her two siblings and their spouses. "No problem," she said, but something had the normally unemotional Marianne, daughter of First Lady Dorothy Haynes, sounding rattled. Mother tilted her head and fingered the family pictures on the mantel above the fireplace.

Sharonda moved to her side. "Mother, what's wrong?"

She sniffed as she picked up the ornate wooden frame with a younger version of Grandpa, the late Diocesan Bishop Joseph Haynes. "One

96

day..." Mother carried the photo over to the coffee table and gingerly placed it next to the picture where she, Sharonda, and her siblings sat bundled in Sunday coats.

"I've always wondered, why doesn't Grandma have a copy of your wedding picture on the wall?"

"I never will." Grandma hobbled into the living room. "He's the mistake I pray you don't repeat, Sharonda. Your mother's always pushing to make that father of yours into something he's not."

"That's enough, Mom. Or do you want me to cut this visit short?" Marianne Peterson turned and glared at Sharonda. "And close your mouth."

"Yes, ma'am." Sharonda lowered her gaze.

Grandma shuffled over to her La-Z-Boy, covered her legs with the throw, and nestled in with a crossword puzzle. "What did I do to get the honor of your attention?"

"Mom, I'd come more often, but you have so many stipulations for my visits." Mother lifted a finger. "Don't bring my husband." Another finger. "Call if it's a weekday because they have scheduled events for you here." Another. "Movie night. Field trips. Grocery day. Water aerobics. Have I missed anything?" She held up six fingers.

"You hungry?" Grandma focused on Sharonda. "Not that you've missed any meals."

Sharonda clenched her fist.

Mother stepped in front of her like a human shield. "Any rocks you have to throw, aim them at me. Not my child."

"I'm okay," Sharonda said, knowing she was anything *but* okay.

"Lena called." Mother remained a protective wall.

"She needs to mind her own business," Grandma scolded.

Mother took a deep breath and exhaled. "Is it true?"

"Can't live forever. Joseph's been waiting a long time." Grandma looked toward the mantel.

"But to deny treatment. Come on, Mom. If not for me, then consider your other children. Grandchildren."

Grandma penciled something in her puzzle book. "I've lived my life. Made my place in this world. Y'all still working at it and that takes time. My body is tired. I'm not interested in radiation. It will only prolong the inevitable."

Mother placed a fisted hand on her hip. "You're God now?"

"Don't be stupid. I would never presume such authority. If God chooses to heal me, fine. I'm just not willing to involve a physician."

"God works through doctors," Mother countered.

"Go home, Marianne. I've said all I'm going to say on this." Grandma raised her voice. "You've done enough already."

Mother jerked, losing her distinguishing erect pose.

Sharonda placed a hand on her arm. "Grandma needs her rest."

"You drive." Mother stormed out of the apartment.

The ride home was quieter than the journey there. Mother stared out the window.

Dad will know what to do. Sharonda had never been so glad to pull into their garage. "Mother?"

She simply stared ahead with her hands folded in her lap.

"Mother." *Lord God, help her. I don't know what to do.* "Mama, please answer me." Sharonda shook her arm.

Tears flowed down Mother's cheeks. Her entire body jerked against her sobs.

Sharonda ran into the house screaming, "Daddy, Mama needs you."

❧

The sound of the kitchen door interrupted Sharonda's prayers. The entire day had passed, and night had come. Her numerous steps, back and forth, could have completed the seven trips around Jericho.

"Your mother is asleep," Dad said.

She embraced him. "Finally."

His iron posture bowed. He held her for a long hug. "What happened at Grandma's?"

Sharonda stepped back and studied the fatigue that plagued his face.

He nodded and encouraged her with a squeeze to the shoulder.

"It started yesterday. Mother got a call from Grandma's friend, Ms. Lena."

"Hold up. Make an old man some coffee as we talk, please."

"Yes, sir." Sharonda covered his hand with hers for a moment, then walked to the cabinet and found the grounds.

Dad sat at the table, his head cradled in his hands.

"I never should've opened my mouth." She headed to the sink.

"What did you say?"

She filled the coffee pot. "Grandma walked in on me asking Mother why there were no wedding pictures of you two."

Dad groaned and lifted his head. "Did you receive an answer?"

"Just that ... I shouldn't make the same mistakes as Mother." She studied his face and his body language. "Something about her trying to make you into someone you're not." Sharonda settled the pot onto the burner.

"Is that all?"

"No. When Grandma made a comment about me not missing a meal, Mother took up for me. You should have seen her, Dad. She stood between me and Grandma as if she were the Great Wall of China." Her throat grew thick with emotion.

"You say that as if you'd expect otherwise. Your mother loves you, Sharonda." He took the mug of black coffee she'd prepared. "I see you poured two. Go get your cup and let's talk."

She dumped plenty of sugar and evaporated milk in hers and hurried back to the table.

Dad took several sips. "Your mother's troubles go way back. Before you were even born. I've always loved her. She wasn't studdin' me, then." He stared into his cup.

"Studying you?" Sharonda corrected him.

He chuckled. "No, studdin' is the way my daddy used to say it. She didn't pay me any attention. Or think about me past a common greeting to a neighbor. Never considered me long enough to matter. It's probably why I wanted her so bad. No girl had ever ignored my advances." He looked up. "But she wasn't mine to love. Charles Mitchell, handpicked by her father and his, had spoken for her."

Sharonda moved to the edge of her seat. She took a swallow of the hot drink, some of the coffee dripping down her chin. "That wouldn't happen to be Diocesan Mitchell by any chance?"

Dad handed her a paper towel. "One and the same."

"You said, 'spoken for.' As in engaged?"

"In my time, pastors paired up their children, especially those being groomed to take over the ministry. So, I wouldn't call it a formal engagement your mother had accepted, but an understanding she went along with. Charles came to town with his father a few times a year. He did more preaching than pursuing your mother, thus a long engagement." He sipped his coffee.

Too much of this story sounded like her life now. Sharonda fidgeted. "If she wasn't 'studdin you,' how did you two become an item?"

"Many years later. I was eighteen. She'd gone off to college and returned a schoolteacher." He placed his World's Greatest Dad cup on the coaster. "In our case, separation did indeed make our hearts grow fonder. Gave me time to become a man and work with my father in the ministry."

"That's when you and Mother fell in love?"

He shook his head. "No. She considered my interest puppy love. She swore the euphoria of being with an older woman would go away." His face grew solemn. "It didn't, but grew stronger. And she grew sadder the closer the day came to marry Charles. I made it a point to be there for her. To listen. To comfort her. Charles didn't want a partner in ministry, he wanted a trophy wife. A personal assistant, free to travel and be dedicated to his vision."

Sharonda toyed with her necklace. "Y'all fell in love."

He nodded. "Time and time again, I went to her father. He wouldn't budge. His daughter was to marry Charles Mitchell." He leaned back in his seat and sighed. "I'd only meant to say goodbye. Our last secret meeting I thought I could have one kiss to take with me and make it last a lifetime. One led to another. Until nothing else was left." He stared into his cup.

Her chest tightened. Sharonda's night with Carl Ray ... A feeling as close to shame as she'd ever experienced lodged in the back of her mind.

"When her father found out she was pregnant with your brother Travis, he demanded we marry. Not that I ever felt forced. Your mother was all I'd ever wanted. Then Marianne supported my desire to quit working at the chicken warehouse and attend seminary. Their daughter becoming the breadwinner didn't endear me to her parents."

He ran a hand over his head. "After school, my father still wouldn't let me in the pulpit. Acting outside the will of God came at a price. For years, no preaching. My father sentenced me to sit on the front row, observe, and learn with a repentant heart. They called it a sit down. I served and earned the respect of my elders, my peers, and the congregation. Charles and I are friends today because of it. Humbleness and a contrite spirit for the sins we commit go a long way."

Sharonda toyed with a cork-padded coaster, unable to look at her father. "Do you regret marrying Mother?"

"Never." Spittle sprayed, he spoke with such force. "Your grandpa died of a massive heart attack within hours of contacting Charles' father and calling off the wedding. Grandma blames your mother." He sighed. "And punishes me."

Sharonda gasped, sloshing coffee over the rim of her cup. "I didn't know."

Dad patted her hand. "I haven't seen your mother this depressed in a long time. Am I missing something?"

"Grandma refuses to have radiation. I never heard what for, just that Grandma wouldn't prolong the inevitable."

He scrubbed his jaw. "Joseph Haynes died thirty-three years ago this month ... and a part of your mother did, too. If Lady Haynes dies with things the way they are now, I fear Marianne will forever harbor guilt for loving me. She tries too hard to fix things. I fear she'll eventually break." Dad gripped his coffee mug. "I take full responsibility."

"Will she be all right?"

"Janice picked up her prescription while she was out. I'm praying. And your mother, for the most part, is a strong woman. It's my job to take care of her, even when she doesn't know she needs my strength. Pray for her."

He stood and pushed his chair back. "You're so much like your mother." Dad squeezed her shoulder. "Good night, baby."

"Dad, what about the meeting tomorrow? Carl and I have an idea we feel will bring the community together in unity."

"I'm cancelling. My wife needs me."

"But Mother is adamant about you receiving the appointment as Suffragan bishop."

"She means well. One thing I know, if and when God elevates me, it will be in His perfect timing. In His blessings, He adds no sorrow. Sharonda, always question your motives. Me becoming the next bishop will not resurrect your grandpa from the dead, absolve your mother's guilt, or bridge the gap in her relationship with her mother. Only God can do that. We just have to realize that it's not about us. If you take anything away from this situation, learn to ask God for a humble and contrite spirit." He bent and kissed the top of her head before he retired for the night.

Sharonda cleared their cups from the table. Mother's story could have been hers. Marianne Peterson might be prim and proper but she made mistakes. So many of her mother's ways made more sense. Like Dad, she'd take better care of her mother. Be *her* wall.

She knew she shouldn't desire to rekindle the possibilities of a relationship with Carl Ray and stress Mother further. And Dad's portrayal of a contrite spirit wouldn't be silenced.

For too long, she'd been ruled by her feelings, not caring how her decisions affected others. She didn't want to be the source of the kind of pain she witnessed in her grandmother's apartment. The kind that tore families apart. However, disaster was imminent if she continued to live as she had for the past fourteen years.

Help me.

Chapter Thirteen

Sharonda loaded the binding machine in the church's central copy room. "It's been over a week since the fight with Grandma. Mother spends most of her day locked away in her room. I'm worried about her."

Carl Ray laid the Sunday curriculum she'd compiled for him on the counter and crossed to her side of the worktable. "We don't have to do this today."

She yanked the arm down on the machine, causing the coil to miss some of the holes. "No, I need to keep busy."

He bumped her hip with his. "Move over, I'll finish the binding. We don't want the spines to come out crooked. You can hand me the coils."

Sharonda offered him the plastic from the case, careful not to make contact with his hands and his long, graceful—yet strong—fingers able to coax the notes on his keyboard into submission.

Focus.

She touched the base of her neck and sighed. "Mother has lost weight. Barely speaks to any of us." She prepped another coil. "I hear Dad praying in his office late at night. His clothes are sagging from his tall frame. I believe he's fasting, but Mother's hollow cheeks make her appear to be starving."

"Your mother is strong." He added the finished booklet to the pile.

"You sound like Dad." She slapped her palms on the table. "But a week? The strongest women need food."

Carl Ray turned his warm brown eyes on her. "Yeah, but you said it yourself. She's fighting with your grandma, grieving your grandpa, and wrestling with her past. That's enough to make anyone sad."

"It's beyond sadness. I didn't think people like Mother or Daddy could be depressed."

He cocked his head. "Why? Because they're in church leadership? We live in a fallen world."

Sharonda punched him in the arm. "Are you making fun of me?"

"You act as if the calling on their lives is some protective shield. We're not immune. Our bodies, our minds, they fail. You have to take comfort in God."

"I guess I'm more surprised than anything … and scared." The back of her throat tightened. "That shell of a woman is *not* my mother. I never thought I'd say this, but I'd rather have the old Marianne Peterson, speaking her mind, demanding things to be her way or no way. I've been so mad having horrible thoughts toward the woman, but I never wanted her to be sick."

Carl Ray took the binding from her and laid it on the counter. "Come here."

Sharonda buried her face against his chest. The heat of his body. The weight of his arms. The beat of his heart. Strength.

He leaned back and peered into her eyes. "Everything is going to work together for the good. Now I understand your mother's protectiveness toward you that day in your office. Their story could've been ours. I should have protected you." The dreaded apology lurked within the fibers of his empathy-filled voice.

She bristled. "You don't owe me anything. But if you must make your confession, I'll listen."

"Shhh." He rested his head atop hers. "Right now, I'm Superman and you're the beauty in distress. Play along."

If he only knew. Play-along could be her middle name.

"And when I'm down"—he lifted his head and gazed into her eyes again—"you can be my Superwoman. Until then, let me love you." He cupped her chin.

"Not because I owe you an apology." His head lowered. "I want to live life with my best friend."

She whispered, "It's *best* we leave things the way they are."

"I don't believe you."

Did he see the effects of hope's first blossoms taking root in her heart? His breath warmed her face. His lips hovered within her reach. Tremors coursed through her body. She closed her eyes.

Nothing.

Sharonda pushed off his chest.

He encircled her inside his arms before she could get away. "Where are you going?"

"We have work to do."

"You're the one who said I could apologize. I want to do that *before* I kiss you real good."

She shook her head and pressed her balled fists against his chest. "You've got me so confused."

Carl Ray laughed. "For someone who's supposed to be Pastor Peterson's quiet daughter, you sure talk a lot. It's a good thing I'm a patient man."

"Grrr." She tried to wiggle out of his embrace.

He settled his head at the bend of her neck and pulled her into a deeper hug. "Forgive me, Sharonda."

She stilled.

"I took what did not belong to me. You deserved more. I sinned. God has forgiven me. Now, I ask you. Forgive me for leaving you behind."

His remorse—so similar to King David's—nagged her. He raised his head, then leaned in a second time. Anything that wasn't Carl Ray became white noise. "I love you, Sharonda Peterson. From this day forward, I ask that you go where I go. That my God be your God."

Her God *was* his God. Long-standing insecurities vanished. She raised her lips to his hovering within her reach.

He pulled back. "I'm waiting."

She blinked. What in the world?

He kissed her bottom lip and she wrapped her arms around his neck to draw him closer, but he leaned back. "Not until I know your heart. Are you ready to fight at my side for the rest of our lives?"

"What are you saying, Carl Ray?"

He tilted his head to the side. "I want you to exchange our one night for a lifetime. Will you marry me?"

Mother will object. "I love you, Carl Ray."

"But?" He released her. Lines stretched across his forehead and creased the corners of his mouth.

Sharonda ducked her head. Where his arms had been, a chill wrapped around her like an invisible rope. She hugged herself. "I *do* love you."

"That's not what I asked." He walked to the binding machine.

Sharonda followed and slid her arms around his waist from behind. How could she please everyone? When he didn't respond, she rested her head on his back and tightened her hug.

"I want to be your wife more than anything ..." *It's just not the right—*

"That's what I'm talking about." He whipped around and claimed her mouth, swallowing her misgivings.

He tasted sweeter than the heart of a ripe, red watermelon. She drew closer.

Carl Ray raised his head. "Hey, girl, you can't brush up on me like that." He pecked her on the cheek and moved to the other side of the table. "Soon, my love." He gave her a playful wink. "I'm hoping you're not wanting a long engagement."

He looked so happy, she didn't have the heart to tell him he'd misunderstood her.

Again.

❧

"He loves me." In the church parking lot, Sharonda flung the curriculum over the console and into the passenger seat, and climbed into the SUV. Away from Carl Ray, reality settled in. *How does a girl go from unwanted to possibly engaged, then into a mistaken engagement?*

As if someone uncapped the pressure valve on a fire hydrant, tears sprang forth. "Why do things have to be so complicated?"

What if she talked to her mother? No, that might push her too far.

Sharonda needed to speak with Brice. But the ever-absentee pastor said he'd contact her and she'd respect his request.

Too many changes. Too little time. But ... Carl Ray loved her.

Why now?

Her phone vibrated in her purse. Sharonda snagged a couple napkins. She blew, then answered the call.

"Hey, Sis." Travis's booming voice struck a wrong chord.

She held the cell away from her ear.

"Sharonda?"

She pinched the bridge of her nose. "What's up?"

"Thought you'd be glad to hear from me."

"I am." She sniffed.

"Just wanted to say thanks."

"Huh?"

"You sick?"

"You were saying?"

"Dad called. Told me how you spoke up for me. Things must be really bad at the church."

She rubbed her temple. "I wouldn't say that."

"With Mom sick, he finally asked me to come home." He bulldozed through her sigh. "I promised Dad I'd learned my lesson. The baby wasn't even mine. Cheryl lied. Did Dad tell you that?"

"No."

"Well, after I give my formal apology to our fellowship, I get my band back. I miss the boys. I gave Victory Temple Church two weeks' notice. However, if they can't get a replacement by then, I agreed to stay on longer."

"Why did they let you play for them without a reference from your last church?"

"They needed a musician and left it up to me to work out my soul's salvation."

Maybe it was the lack of remorse in his tone that grated on her nerves. Sharonda pressed her palm against her forehead and tried to release the growing tension.

Under Carl Ray's leadership, Sunday morning worship song selections revealed who God was and all He'd done. No more of Travis's long, redundant solos about getting your blessings—loud for the sake of being loud.

What have I done?

❧

Sunday, Carl walked into the Youth Building's smaller chapel where children's church had convened hours earlier. He'd waited out the last of the staff members, not wanting any talebearers to guess his destination.

How long must they hide their relationship? Over a month had gone by since he popped the question and Sharonda still insisted Mother Peterson needed time to recover. His heart ached with repressed love. If only he'd realized the depth of his feelings that first Sunday on the job. She stood at the whiteboard in her classroom.

He slipped inside and wrapped his arms around her waist. "I've waited all day to hold you."

Sharonda turned and faced him. "Haven't you had enough of people walking in on us?" She put a measure of sternness in her words, but her smile let him know she liked his embrace.

"Say the word and I'll ask your dad's permission to marry you today. Then we won't have to hide anymore. I want the world to know." He twirled Sharonda around.

She giggled and melted against him.

"Have dinner with me, warm vanilla and berries."

"What? Is that my new nickname?"

"It's your signature scent." Carl sniffed her neck. To have and to hold took on deeper meaning—from this day and forever. "I want to celebrate with you, among other things. We never celebrated our engagement."

"I can't today. Mother is recovering, but she's still on the mend. Service wears her out. I promised Dad I'd hang around the house while he makes hospital visits."

"Fine, I'll join you there. Maybe I can have the talk with him after dinner." Carl nuzzled the spot on her neck, and she offered her sweet kiss like he knew she would.

Carl stepped back. "How is it that now we're an official couple, I can't get a date?"

She looked toward the door.

"What's wrong?"

"Are we sure we want to have the talk with Dad tonight?"

He crossed his arms. "Have you changed your mind?"

"I want your meeting with Dad to go smoothly. Especially after everything happened with Mother." She still hadn't looked at him.

More suitable type. Other offers. Her mother's words from the day in Sharonda's office crept through the alcoves of his mind. How big a hold did Lady Peterson have over Sharonda?

He frowned. "What are you *not* saying?" Had she cut ties with preacher man? "Come here, girl, empty arms make me feel vulnerable."

She stepped into his embrace and laid her hand on his chest, making her mother's words fade from his thoughts. "It's bad timing, but you never have to doubt my love for you."

Speak now or forever hold your peace. Wouldn't she have told him by now if she'd changed her mind?

"You came in here ready to celebrate. What's the occasion?"

"Us, for one. The booklets are a hit. We make an awesome team. The things we'll do in ministry together, I can't wait. I could tell they listened in class this morning, and even Aaron stayed awake. That's important. Aaron's the kind of guy everyone wants to follow. He's got the *It* factor."

"Which lesson did you cover?" Adoration shone in her brown eyes.

He stroked her cheek. "I opened the class asking who all were saved. How that's more than a one-time verbal commitment, but a daily surrendering of oneself to God." He grazed her lips with his. "Speaking of … I got a call Friday to renew my contract, but I'm more concerned with what I'm doing here. Working with you and these kids is a game changer."

111

"What if my parents withhold their blessings?" She turned toward the whiteboard and placed the marker she held in the tray.

He shook his head. "They won't."

"What makes you so sure?"

"All I have to do is prove to them you mean more to me than my music career. I'll give it all up for you. I love what I do here at the church. I've been mentoring Derrick. He's really growing in the Lord. Got him a gig with one of my buddies' gospel jazz groups. No more club life."

"That's great, but I don't want you to turn your back on your dreams and resent loving me later. Leave the band to Travis. You've done more than your part with the musicians. You wouldn't want any regrets."

"I can make music wherever I go."

"You say that now. My mother is suffering because she chose my dad, going against her parents' wishes. The guilt is killing her."

"She loves your dad. Y'all have a beautiful family. Pastor said it today in service. This trial will pass. Together, nothing else matters."

"Is love enough?"

"It must be." He banged his fist against the whiteboard.

She jumped.

He stuffed his hands in his pockets. "No one said it would be easy. This morning at church, Marianne Peterson stood at her husband's side. Showing up when she's at her weakest, fighting for what they have. I'm ready to fight for us. Are you?"

"Carl Ray, please don't be upset with me." She chewed her bottom lip. "I don't know how to fight. And then there's Travis."

"What about your brother?"

Her wary gaze pierced his heart. She rocked from side to side. "I try so hard to please everybody."

"Shhh." He grabbed her hands, pulling her away from the board. "You just need more time. I didn't come here to upset you. Take care of your mother tonight and plan to spend the day with me tomorrow celebrating. I'll be at your office to pick you up at ten in the morning. Make your excuses. You'll be gone for the day."

"Okay." She looked into his eyes. Vulnerability shone in their depths, yet she seemed to trust him.

That familiar ache filled his chest. "If I kiss you, I won't stop. And you already said you can't fight." He moved behind the closest chair.

She took a step toward him.

Carl gripped the back. "Seriously, open that door. Better yet, get your purse and go."

"Really?" A sly smile lit her face.

"Go."

"Aye, aye, Captain." She headed to the door, her hips swinging.

"Hurry."

Chapter Fourteen

Carl laughed and passed the phone across the table to Derrick. A waitress pulled a pen from behind her ear and cleared her throat. She tucked escaped strands of gray back into the bun at the nape of her neck.

"I'm sorry, ma'am," Carl offered. "Just showing my boy the latest comedian who's gone viral on Facebook."

"No problem, youngster." She gave Carl a gap-toothed smile. "What can I get for you?"

"The All-Star breakfast."

She shifted her weight and angled toward Derrick. "And you?"

"Same thing."

"More coffee?"

Carl lifted a finger. "That's a yes for me."

Derrick covered the rim of the off-white mug. Dr Pepper, please, ma'am."

"Good to see young folks with manners. I'll drop off this order and be right back with your drinks." She walked to the counter, a slight limp in her steps.

"Like I was saying—"

A woman slid into the booth next to Carl. Her cloying perfume reminded him of cotton candy.

"Excuse me?" Carl inched over.

She scooted closer.

Derrick snickered. "Should we know you, beautiful?"

She couldn't be more than twenty, but her boldness added a few years.

The waitress returned and set Derrick's soda in front of him. "Do I need to get your drink order, Missy?" She poured Carl's coffee.

The young woman glanced over her shoulders. "Yes."

"No." Carl scooted against the wall.

The intruder took a folded piece of paper and slid it underneath his plate. "I stopped by to leave you my number."

The waitress tisked. "Gal, ain't your mama taught you a man likes a chase? Too forward these days. Learn some etiquette, then maybe you can win the eye of some fine gentlemen. But this is a place of business."

Carl smiled at the waitress's gentle yet firm ways.

The stranger narrowed her eyes. "I'm only having a little fun. Plus, it was a bet." She hopped up and joined a group of young ladies at a corner table.

Carl read his rescuer's name tag. "Ms. Erma, thank you."

"You're welcome, honey. These young gals don't have no home training no more."

Derrick laid his head on the table and enjoyed a belly-jiggling laugh.

"Now if you could school this one"—Carl crooked his thumb in Derrick's direction—"I'll forever be in your debt."

Ms. Erma grinned. "Let me check on your food before her home-girls get brave enough to come have their encounter with you, Mr. Everhart." She winked.

Another fan? "I owe you."

"Nope. Just doing my Christian duty. Keep serving the Lord. Enjoying your worship at the church." A sister in Christ, even better.

"Pray for me. I truly desire to serve Him well."

"I can tell. And we, the church body, have to rally together to keep the enemy away." Ms. Erma nodded toward the young ladies' table.

They all laughed.

The bell at the counter sounded.

"Breakfast, comin' right up." Erma returned and set steaming plates before them with a heated carafe of syrup.

They ripped into waffles, shoved eggs into their mouths, and followed with a bite of crisp bacon.

After Carl downed the last of his hash browns, he leaned back, patting his stomach. "That's what I'm talking about. Invigorating game of basketball at the church, followed by a big breakfast. Winning makes it even better."

"Been meaning to ask. Is there a particular reason you jump away from a beautiful woman like she's got cooties?"

Derrick waved at the young ladies before addressing Carl again. "I haven't seen any progress with the pastor's daughter, but I watch you dodging the eligibles at the church. Are you hiding something?"

"What are you implying?" Carl took a sip of his coffee.

Derrick placed his forearms on the table and leaned in. "You keep teaching how being God's man is more than sitting on a pew, reciting Scripture. Got to have some fruit. If your fruit is leaning toward men, then it's gone astray, spoiled on the vine, fell out the tree—however you want to say it. It's in opposition to His Word and your deeds aren't adding up." He ended with a definitive nod.

Carl chuckled. "What if I was? Would you know how to lead me to Christ with the Scriptures?"

Derrick coughed. "I ain't gon' lie. That whole situation makes me uncomfortable. I'd probably avoid you."

"It's our natural response to steer clear of things we don't understand. But one thing I know, we are all in need of a Savior. Avoiding your neighbor doesn't sound like loving him, and that's in His Word too." Carl stacked his empty dishes. "I'll have to add that to our studies. I want to make sure we're equipped to be effective witnesses if the opportunity ever presents itself." He sat back. "To answer your question, I'm engaged to be married. By the end of the day, she'll be wearing my ring."

Derrick threw a wadded napkin at him. "Man, quit playing. How come I ain't never seen you with this mystery woman since you been here."

"But you have. Think."

Derrick frowned.

"We're together almost every day."

"What does she look like?"

Carl smiled. "Long hair, when she straightens it. About my complexion. Smells of vanilla and berries. Mmmm."

"Come on, man, I ain't going around sniffing women like some neighborhood hound."

"She's beautiful. Long lashes. Thick in the chest and hips. Smart."

Ms. Erma approached. "Can I clear your plates?"

"Yes, ma'am." Carl handed her his dishes.

Derrick's followed. "Sharonda?"

"It took you long enough."

"Congratulations! You'd think her mother would be running around telling everybody, introducing you as Sharonda's future."

Carl grimaced.

"Wait." He turned his eyes upward as if flipping a mental Rolodex. Then, he snapped his fingers. "When did all this take place? Didn't Pastor McDowel introduce himself as her fiancé that night we ran into them at the restaurant? I feel you're a better choice. The preacher is a little too clean if you ask me. Brows manicured better than the church's lawn. Even his lips keep a shine to them. A real pretty boy. Don't get me wrong."

"I'm listening."

"I don't know if I should," Derrick said.

Carl placed his forearms on the table, then leaned toward his friend. "Tell me this, did you know about their engagement before that night? Ever see them interact?"

"Nope, but I know her momma wanted the match. Always making comments about how the two churches would benefit if they came together. I overlooked the possibility considering McDowel's age. Sharonda never showed too much interest that I could see. But I could've missed the signs in all the hype surrounding his visits. When will y'all make the big announcement?"

Carl gripped the back of his neck. "It's complicated."

"Huh. You better make sure you have First Lady's blessing. Sharonda does anything her mother tells her to do."

"I'm waiting to ask Pastor for her hand properly."

Derrick shook his head. "If you haven't asked the father, then why present her with a ring today?"

Carl clamped his mouth shut.

"Hey, man, forget I said anything." Derrick pulled his wallet out and laid a ten on the table. "I like the happy Carl. By the way, this should make you feel better. My sister says things are improving at home. She and Aaron are supposed to come to church as a family."

"Man, that's great."

"Yeah, she's been through a lot. Works two jobs. The fact Aaron can't read limits his ability to get any good employment. Playing by ear only gets you so far."

Carl fished in his pocket for his wallet. "I never would've known."

"He's good at hiding his limitation. But with the way you break things down and give examples of how the Bible applies to our every-day decisions, he's learning." The drummer tapped his chest. "It gets you right here. The message burrows deep and makes you uncomfortable, but in a good way."

Carl nodded. He'd never take credit for what God was doing, but to be a part of the process … "I got to get out of here. I need to call my agent before I meet with Sharonda."

Carl scooted to the end and extended his leg to work the kinks from his knees. "Thanks for sharing."

Derrick slid out the booth. "Take my hand, old man."

"You weren't saying that when I ran you up and down the court this morning."

"Ahh. Maybe your next lesson should cover humility." Derrick slapped him on the back.

"Maybe."

"Forget what I said about Sharonda."

"No. You were right to ask questions. Could be I've rushed things."

⁓

Sharonda hurried into her office after spending too much time primping. Carl Ray should've told her where they were going.

He swiveled around in her desk chair and stood when she entered.

She ran a finger beneath her puffy eyes. "I have twelve minutes. You said ten o'clock." He crossed the room toward her.

What a beautiful man. His crisp, white shirt—monogrammed at the cuff—contoured his chest. The stitching running the length of his jeans screamed designer. Italian loafers completed his outfit. Wherever they were going must be important.

He took the box of candy and the card from her hand. "My favorite."

Sharonda plucked the chocolate from his clutches and gave a gentle slap to his hand. "That's not for you."

He rubbed the back of his knuckles. "That's what I get for assuming."

"It's no big deal." She ambled to her desk.

Carl walked to the wall behind her that held her degrees. "What had you hoped to do with your doctorate?"

"Teach. Research. Family therapy. Anything in those areas."

"Why didn't you?" He handed her the card.

"Is something wrong?" She glanced at her watch as she placed the envelope on a stack of papers. "I thought we had to leave at ten."

"Why didn't you become a teacher? Do research? Or practice family therapy?"

Sharonda closed the distance and wrapped her arms around his waist. "Where did all this come from?"

He moved out of her embrace. "It's a simple question."

"I do all those things here."

"Why, because your mother told you to? If she tells you to marry Brice, will you?" He folded his arms.

"Baby, you're scaring me." She cupped his jaw. "I teach. All curriculum used at New Hope is my research. And I practice family therapy with the youth and their families on a daily basis. Even now, I have to address an issue of promiscuity that's been brought to my attention. The box of candy you were about to eat is for her."

He leaned into her touch and wrapped his arms around her. "What am I going to do with you?"

She kissed his nose. "I've been wondering all morning. You could've given me a hint on how to dress."

He nuzzled her neck. "Why the chocolate?"

Sharonda squirmed, giggling. "Some messages need to be served with a measure of sweetness. And the card is a keepsake to remind her I really care, even if I say things she may not want to hear."

"You're so smart. And beautiful. Wait, something's different." He backed away and searched her face as if he hunted clues. His gaze traveled her body.

Under the spell of his appreciation, Sharonda spun around in a circle.

"Again." He took and held her hand above her head like a dance partner. "You're thinner."

Though cautious, she turned, encouraged by his slow smile. "You play too much."

"Not when it comes to you."

She ducked her head. "Thank you."

He drew her to his chest, then lifted her chin. "Cute or not, you'll have to change clothes. Ruffles and linen don't belong in New York City in September. You'll want jeans and a jacket after the sun goes down. It can get pretty chilly."

"That's where you're taking me?" She squealed. "Hold up, I can't drop everything and leave. I have responsibilities."

"And I thought I was one of them," he countered. "I want to romance the love of my life. It's one day. Come on, Sharonda."

"I'd need to run home to pack and change clothes."

"Nope. We return today and Janice already picked out some outfits."

"Oh, wow. You thought of everything. How did you convince her?"

"Shopping spree."

"You mean she's going with us? I thought you said *romantic*. This is turning into a family affair."

He kissed her forehead. "We *need* a chaperone."

121

She sighed. "Yeah."

"I have a meeting with my agent. You can shop with your sister or hang out at my place. Then, I plan to wine and dine you at my favorite steakhouse."

"When do we leave?"

He released her hand and pulled her earlobe. "As soon as I get us to Skyway Drive and we board the jet. Janice is meeting us there."

Fly. New York City. Fancy dining. "Your new lifestyle is so fast-paced. Are you sure you'll be happy settling down in Longview?"

"That came out of nowhere." Dryness entered his tone. "I thought you'd enjoy spending time with me, getting away for a change."

"I will. I'm used to planning things out. And there's Mother. If both Janice and I are gone and Dad needs help, then what?"

"We can always skip dinner for the sake of time and come home early."

⁂

Carl guided Sharonda inside his high-rise apartment on Madison Avenue. "What do you think?"

"Pardon me, love birds. This girl has got to visit the ladies' room." Janice crossed her ankles.

"Down that hall, second door to the right."

She zipped past, trailing her luggage. "Don't mind me. I'm going to spruce up a bit. No telling who a girl might run into."

"Exquisite view." Sharonda took his hand and pulled him toward the eleven-foot, floor-to-ceiling, windows. "I've never seen anything so grand."

"Me, neither." He studied Sharonda and soaked up her wonder and awe. Until now, his success never had meaning. "Let me show you around."

She beamed. "Lead the way."

With her here, in this space, it felt more like a home than a rental for the first time. She embodied prism colors he'd never noticed missing from his pristine light-gray décor. He planted a chaste kiss on her lips.

Sharonda closed her eyes.

Boy, she didn't make things easy. He waited until she opened them and gave him that shy smile of hers. Carl waved a hand through the air. "What you see is what you get. It's an open concept. The two bedrooms have en suites. You can tour those while I'm at my meeting." He moved to stand behind her, wrapping his arms around her waist as she watched the city. "This is a corner residence giving you south and east exposure."

"How many floors?" Amazement dripped from her words.

"We're on the thirtieth, but there's a total of thirty-four."

She tapped the glass. "The Empire State Building is your view. This place is costing you a fortune."

"Your response is priceless. Maybe it's a good thing I'll have this place for a while longer."

She turned in his arms. "Why the meeting with your agent all of a sudden?"

He checked his watch. "I have to go. Terry is the concierge. The buttons are labeled in the kitchen on the wall. Press, it rings his station, and he'll help you with any needs you can think of. I'll have my cell on me too." He leaned close and sniffed. "Nap. Make sure to lie on my pillow. I want this scent in my dreams."

She pushed at his chest. "I thought we were returning home today."

"Don't worry. I'll have you home in plenty of time. I'm taking the pillow with me." He kissed her pouting mouth.

"Excuse me," Janice interrupted.

They parted.

"Don't forget you still have to drop me off." She waltzed into the living area to stand next to the leather lounger. The sleek, long jacket paired with jeans and boots made her look like a native to the city. "Sharonda, if you're going shopping with me, you better hurry and change."

"No. I think I'll shower and take my time getting ready for tonight."

He gathered his satchel and shades. "More like you want time to snoop in my apartment while I'm gone."

She gave him a sassy grin. "What if I do?"

"Have at it. There's nothing to find. My agent had most of my things moved to storage for safekeeping."

Janice walked toward the door. "Let's go before you're late."

"All right, all right." He blew Sharonda a kiss and followed.

Chapter Fifteen

Sharonda crossed over to the corner window. People wandered the concrete walkways and cars populated the city streets below; yet, thick silence prevailed in Carl Ray's apartment high above the action.

She wasn't a big-city girl. Would he get bored and compare her to the women in his world? Would he resent her for wanting to stay in Texas?

Stop. He loves you.

In the kitchen, Sharonda ran a finger along the length of the granite counter. How long had he known about this meeting? Maybe he really wanted to return to the stage, but not the city life he'd complained about. By marrying her, he'd bring a little home back with him and get the best of both worlds.

Sharonda covered her ears and hummed over the voices in her head. She worked her way to the oversized lounger, nabbed a magazine, and reclined. Would this be their life? Him gone, leaving her behind? "Stop thinking so hard."

Sharonda scrubbed both hands up and down her arms.

Her cell buzzed. She hopped up to snag the phone from the coffee table. Reading Carl Ray's **I love u** text message shooed away the rising doubts long enough for her to remember the clothes Janice had left in the bathroom.

Black skinny jeans, a blue polka dot blouse, and a yellow jacket hung from the shower rod. Janice had done well. Not only did her sister coordinate her favorite color but the toiletry bag held Sharonda's makeup. Not that she wore it often, but a date with Carl Ray called for the extra effort.

Showered and dressed, Sharonda twirled. She liked how the blouse measured to her hips but flared out at the waistline. Her reflection in the glass didn't show her body thinning enough to leave plus sizes anytime soon. To wear her ideal form-fitting wedding gown, she'd need to hire a personal trainer and a nutritionist. Would Carl Ray consider a year engagement too long? Each look they'd shared … each touch … she'd never make a year—let alone Carl Ray. She grinned. "Six months, tops."

Sharonda walked down the hallway into the master suite. A king-sized bed centered against the white brick accent wall. Its charcoal-stained, wooden headboard gave it a certain masculine feel. She quickened her steps and jumped onto the bed Superwoman style. A clean fresh scent engulfed her as the softness contoured her body like a pair of lambskin gloves.

Heaven's clouds must have been stuffed tight inside the mattress—firm, yet soft. She rolled to her back and fluttered her legs in the air, kicked off her flats, and sent them flying. Which side did he sleep on? She flipped and hugged every pillow on the bed. If he wanted to dream her scent, she'd leave it in as many places as possible.

Sharonda peeled the bedding back and crawled beneath the sheets, tugged the weighty comforter up to her neck, and closed her eyes. As Mrs. Carl Ray Everhart, where would they attend church? Would his friends like her? Would he expect her to get a job and use her degree? Is that why he'd been questioning her earlier? She yawned. They had so much to talk about. So many things to sort through.

Sharonda startled awake. It took a moment to gain her bearings. Movement came from the living area. Carl Ray must've returned. She jumped up and ran into his bathroom. There had to be some mouthwash or something in there to freshen up right quick.

"Out!" Carl Ray's voice boomed.

Sharonda stepped to the bedroom door and halted. She stared at the scantily clad intruder who approached *her* man.

"Out!" Carl pointed toward the door. Outrage shook his core like an earthquake.

"I'm sorry. I thought I'd welcome you back." Mia, his agent's secretary, posed on his couch like a Bunny centerfold in her black lingerie and pumps.

"How dare you invade my home." He refused to venture into the room but remained in the entry hallway.

Mia approached, shrouding him in her pungent perfume.

He turned and faced the wall. "Get some clothes on and get out."

Her hand clutched his shoulder. "I thought—"

Carl shrugged off her touch. "That's not possible or you wouldn't be in my apartment."

Ruffling sounded behind him. He didn't turn around to see if she dressed, but waited until the door clicked closed, then walked into the living area.

Hello. How are you? Carl replayed the visit to his agent's office. Did he say or do anything that might've given Mia the impression he'd wanted her advances? No. He barely remembered the introduction. Twice, she offered drinks and he declined.

"Sharonda?" he called.

She stood in front of his bedroom doorway, visibly shaken.

"Baby, it's not what it looks like." In three large strides, he reached for her.

Sharonda shoved him to one side and marched to the oversized seat next to the couch. Seated, she faced the city lights and stared into the distance.

Carl knelt beside her, placing a hand on her knee.

She brushed his touch away without sparing him a glance.

"Baby, please talk to me."

She blinked. Her chin quivered, but she refused to look at him.

His throat tightened. He got up and paced the wide, wood-planked floors. "How do I explain this part of my life? People take liberties. I know it doesn't explain things, but it's the reality of my profession."

"Is she an old fling?" Sharonda barely spoke above a whisper.

Carl approached and knelt again. "She works in my agent's office."

"Is there history there?"

"Nothing sexual." That earned him a head nod.

"You in the habit of handing out your key?"

"My agent has had access to this place since I was hospitalized. He's my next call."

She slumped back, her eyes closed.

Carl stood and plucked his cell from his back pocket. He called his agent.

"Everhart, what's up?"

"Rodney, I'm putting you on speaker."

"Sure. Something wrong?" Papers rustled in the background.

"Mia was up in my place when I came home."

"By the tone of your voice, may I assume she wasn't invited?"

"Do you still have my key?"

"I keep it in the file. Hold on."

Sharonda raised a tentative gaze in his direction.

Carl pointed to his phone and nodded.

"It's missing. That's mad stupid on her part. Son, I'll handle it," Rodney said.

"Appreciate that." Carl ended the call.

"I thought it was you I heard moving around. Not *that*. When I heard—" Her voice cracked. She shook her head. "It's a lot to take in. A lot to compete with." Weariness washed over her face and left the corners of her mouth sagging like her shoulders.

Carl slid in beside her. "There's *no* competition. My heart belongs to you. It always has. Please, let me hold you."

"So, your agent's secretary simply thought to welcome you home? And I thought Vegas was Sin City. How do you live here?"

"That's part of the reason my meeting ran so long." He wrapped an arm around Sharonda's back. Instead of the reassurance he sought, fear skulked up his back when his passionate girl remained robotic to his touch. "This is not how I planned our day. We won't get to do half the things I'd wanted to before we have to fly back."

"What did you discuss with your agent?"

"My contract is up for renewal. My agent is pushing, but I'm not interested. There's the legal matter with me missing the last two performances with Gospel Mania Productions after my surgery. It took all day to get the producer to settle on a monetary amount or accept the same number of guest appearances on a couple other projects scheduled in the future."

"So, you'll be moving back to New York City?"

He shifted a little, resetting Sharonda to keep the ring box from branding a square into his chest. "My answer depends on the outcome of our day."

Sharonda splayed her hand and he laced his fingers through hers. "I've been thinking."

She swallowed. "Being a follower of Christ is more than a one-time verbal commitment, routine Sunday services, or works in the church but a daily surrendering of oneself to God."

"You spent the day focusing on last Sunday's workbook theme for the band?"

Sharonda unlaced her fingers. "I realized what it would mean for me to follow you." She reached for the edge of her blouse. "I'd be surrendering everything I know. My home. You."

He tensed. "Me?"

She pressed a finger across his lips. "Hear me out." She removed her hand. "I'm not sure I can handle this part of your life. And I'm certain I can't live with you giving up your dreams for me. There'd be too many regrets."

He pulled her in closer, but an impenetrable chasm stretched between them.

Sharonda picked at his shirt button. "We work well together. But … as Mrs. Carl Ray Everhart, you're asking me to follow you to empty apartments while you attend meetings, have women throwing themselves at you, forever invading our privacy. I can only imagine how things would be once you're performing again."

Carl held back his desire to fix things.

"After the honeymoon, what then? Look at my parents. They love each other, yet the regret of disappointing her father with their relationship has all but taken Mother's mind. I don't want you to have what-ifs. I don't want them for myself."

"I believe her remorse is centered around *how* they went about their relationship, not loving your father."

She remained silent.

How could he be holding her and she be so far removed? Did she not hear his heart crumbling beneath the weight of her words? Every "I" spoken dealt a crushing blow. When would someone finally fight for him? His own biological mother gave him away at birth. His surgery wasn't enough to get his adoptive parents to return home from their mission trip. How could he expect Sharonda to do more than those who should've loved him most? He slid to the edge of the seat.

"Pray about it. Big decisions aren't made on an empty stomach." But he already sensed her mind was made up.

Chapter Sixteen

Sharonda leaned forward and forced a Sunday morning smile. If only Hat Lady in the pew in front of hers would move so Sharonda could glimpse Carl Ray's face. She slouched in her seat.

Next to Sharonda, Mother sat tall and regal. She embodied her role as the pillar of New Hope, pretty much back to her old self. Mother smacked Sharonda's arm with her decorative fan.

Sharonda sat up, dislodging her lap scarf. The lace-trimmed material slipped to the floor, and she bent to pick it up.

"I want to give honor to all the ministers on the roster, pulpit guests, and friends," Travis's voice filled the sanctuary.

Sharonda fisted the scarf as a cramp seized the pit of her stomach.

He *would* show the one morning she'd arrived late. Dad hadn't spoken a word about his coming. There'd been no time to prepare Carl Ray.

"Sit up. Your brother's here." Mother bounced on her seat in the most undignified manner.

Travis adjusted the mic. He sported extra pounds around the middle. That was fast. Grey streaked his beard and the suit made him look more like Dad. He cleared his throat several times.

"I'm asking that you forgive me." He gripped his shirt over his heart.

I've changed my mind, Lord. Carl Ray is the best man for the job. Sharonda craned her neck, trying to see him, but he remained hidden behind the music stand.

"I've learned my lesson." Travis turned and pointed toward Carl Ray. "When I grow up, I want to be like you. I'd initially returned to walk back into my role as Minister of Music, but I'd be honored to work under your leadership. The band has nothing but good things to say about you. After class this morning, I see why."

Sharonda gripped the edge of the pew. Her brother had been here that long?

Travis motioned for Dad to stand. "Forgive me, Pastor. I rebelled against your chastening. I didn't see it as an act of love then, but I do now." His voice caught.

Sharonda rubbed the corners of her eyes. Her brother's conviction rang through the room, piercing her own heart.

Mother dried her face with a tissue, catching tears, then she covered Sharonda's hand.

"Don't give up on people." Travis made eye contact with Sharonda. "My sister believed in me."

Sharonda tensed. *Please, Lord, don't let Carl Ray hear it like this.*

"Her vote of confidence is one of the reasons I'm back. This time around, it's not about me but what I do for Christ."

The band circled around Travis.

Carl Ray, the last to join the musicians, ambled toward them but stayed outside the circle.

Dad stood, prayed blessings over his son, then opened the altar to anyone who desired prayer. He raved over the benefits of open repentance.

Aaron broke away from the circle and lifted his hand. "I'm asking for forgiveness."

Dad and the band huddled around the bass guitarist. The prideful man from the play had vanished, and a broken one lowered onto his knees and wept. A petite dark-skinned woman walked onto the stage and knelt beside him, stretching her arm over his back.

"Thank you, Lord." Dad raised his hand. "Saints, God is still in the forgiving business. Repent. Turn from your ways and follow Christ. There's nothing in this world more important than your soul. Come. Surrender the old. God's got more in store for you. A new beginning."

Sharonda remained seated while many gathered at the altar.

Aaron hugged and kissed the woman who knelt at his side. His wife? Did she know what went on at some of those productions? Sharonda realized from the way she comforted Aaron, none of that mattered at the moment.

Off to the side, Carl Ray prayed with the youngest band member. They shared a hug, and Carl Ray ended their time with a pound to Paul's shoulder, making his dreads bounce.

He'd made a difference in their lives.

In a room full of people, an atmosphere charged with an energy so intense it had to be the very presence of God's glory, Sharonda sat empty. Confused. Alone.

In all the works she'd done, had anyone's life been changed?

❧

"Aren't you going to join the band at Wings Plus tonight? Carl will be there." Janice slid beside Sharonda on the porch swing in their backyard and set it into motion.

"Nah, Mother might need me." Sharonda sighed.

"Girl, that's why she has a husband. What's up with you and Carl? His puppy-dog gaze followed you out the sanctuary today. At rehearsals, you spend more time sulking in the corners than you do with him or the kids. Plus, I haven't heard you say anything about a date lately."

"We've joined the youth a few times for a bite afterward."

"As a group? That's not a date. Couples need alone time." Janice stopped the swing and looked into her eyes. "Talk to me. Why y'all acting so stiff and formal? This started last month in New York City. I felt something on the flight home, but I tried to give you two your space."

"It's complicated."

"I'm a good listener, remember."

Sharonda hesitated. Janice did have more experience with men. "What do I do if Carl Ray moves back to New York City?"

Janice scrunched her face. "Duh. Go with him. Enjoy the life of the rich and famous."

Sharonda shook her head. "And walk in on a naked woman in his apartment again—not so enjoyable."

Janice jerked the swing to a halt. "What in the world are you talking about?" She gripped Sharonda's hands. "You poor baby. I can't believe it. And here I thought Carl was different."

Sharonda pulled free and slapped Janice's leg.

"Ouch!"

"It's not what you think."

"So, you didn't catch him in bed with another woman?"

"No. See, that's how rumors get started."

Janice blew out a long breath. "Then everything is fine. What are you complaining about now?"

"You'll never understand. We live different lives. I can't deal with a lot of drama, and it follows Carl Ray around in the form of an hourglass figure wearing the sexiest black lingerie known to man. You should have seen her."

"You're not making sense."

"I fell asleep when you were out shopping. I woke up to noise coming from the living room. I walk in on Carl Ray yelling at a half-naked woman on his couch. Flawless dark skin, perfectly shaped body. When she walked to Carl Ray and placed her hands on his back ..." She closed her eyes and willed the vision to leave. "He threw her out. I can't compete with that; she's everything I'm not."

Janice pointed her finger in Sharonda's face. "Exactly. She's *not* you. And that's who Carl Ray wants."

"For now, but how long will that last? The city is too fast, too different. I told him as much when I explained why I couldn't marry him. He hasn't looked at me the same. He suggested that I think about my decision, but he's been avoiding me ever since we returned. I've really messed up this time." Sharonda swallowed the welling tears.

"Wait, you were engaged and didn't tell me?" Janice said.

Sharonda threw an arm over her sister's shoulder. "Forgive me. All I know how to do is hurt the people I love. Carl Ray. Now you. Serving

Mom and Dad is the only thing I seem to excel at. Maybe I only belong here with them."

"So, you plan to cut the rest of us out of your life like you did before? Now *that's* a plan to keep hurting the ones who love you. You need me. If I'd known about the engagement, you wouldn't have messed up the best thing that's ever happened to you." She crossed her arms.

Sharonda hugged Janice. "I've missed this connection between us."

"Too bad you had to go turn into Mother."

Sharonda leaned away to stare at her sister. *Oh, God, help me.*

"Y'all find ways to make yourselves miserable. Both of you have men who love you and you'd rather throw it away than live happy. This mess has got to stop." Janice leaned toward Sharonda until their noses touched. "Promise me you'll at least go to Carl and tell him what you've told me. Let him know your fears. Fight for your man."

Sharonda pulled away, resting against the back of the swing. "You sound like Carl Ray. I don't know how to. I've never fought for anything in my entire life."

"Be vulnerable like Muhammad Ali."

"And what would you know about the old boxer?" Sharonda asked.

"Girl, all kinds of people hang out at the club trading stories with Bartender Joe. He's always talking about the world's *greatest* fighter so I looked him up. I happen to like boxing. Now listen and learn."

Sharonda laughed. "You get on my nerves."

Ali made the rope-a-dope famous. He wouldn't defend himself. He'd lean into the ropes and take his opponents' jabs. While they weakened from throwing punches and missing for the most part, he rested. Then, finished them off." Janice threw two punches in front of herself like a boxer. "Daddy is always telling us not to lean on our own understanding, but God's. Outlast your uncertainties. Knock them out! Then you can come out the winner." She jabbed one more time at an invisible opponent.

"If only Carl Ray would consider making Longview his permanent residence after he fulfills his contract. It's only a couple performances. He seems to like working with the youth. With me." Sharonda smiled.

Janice pushed the swing into motion again. "Unless you talk to him, you'll never know. What about Brice?"

"I need to call. I could never marry him. Whether Carl Ray and I work through this or not, Carl has my heart."

"That's what I'm talking about! Fight for your man. Float like a butterfly, sting like a bee. Rumble, girl, rumble."

∾

The next day, Sharonda rifled through the youth rally presentation packet spread across her desk. For the third time, she scanned notes filled with Carl Ray's suggestions. If Dad approved the tentative program, five of the largest churches along with the smaller congregations in the area would have their youth joining New Hope's community outreach efforts to demonstrate the power of unified love.

Love. It changed everything. She smiled. Today, she'd have her talk with Carl Ray. They could work things out. This was her time to rumble.

"Somebody looks happy." Janice sauntered into Sharonda's office. "I guess you took my advice and let Carl know you want to marry him? When's the wedding? Will you live here or go there?"

"Shhhh!" Sharonda rushed over to close the door. "Not so loud. Mother's here."

"Does it matter? You're going to tell her about you and Carl Ray anyway." Janice plopped down into a wingback chair.

"Not until I've spoken with him and we've set a date." Sharonda returned to her desk.

Janice crossed her legs. "Ooh. I wish I could be there to see his face when you tell him."

"He's going to think I'm crazy. One minute I give him this deep speech about not being able to follow him, and now he's just going to accept I've changed my mind?"

"Yes. Explain how you were in shock. It's not every day a girl wakes up to a lingerie model on her man's couch." Janice cackled.

"You're so rude." Sharonda shook her head. "As soon as I drop off the rally agenda with Dad, I plan to go to the music room and see if Carl Ray's there. If not, I'll call him and ask him to meet me."

Since Carl Ray had re-entered her life, happiness abounded. How had she ever thought to live life without him? Together, they could do anything.

"Yoo-hoo?" Janice uncrossed her legs and stood.

Sharonda startled, snatched up her notes, and pressed them against her chest, silently chiding herself for letting her mind wonder.

"Don't let me hold you up. I need to get to the auditorium and help Derrick and Travis paint the props for the skit. As a matter of fact, I'm late."

Sharonda headed to her father's office. How should she tell Carl Ray? Different scenarios played in her mind. What questions would he have for her? She bumped into someone and teetered off balance. She lifted her gaze from the gray carpet to Carl Ray's face. His hands rested at her waist to steady her.

"Watch yourself." Too soon, he stepped away. "I just finished meeting with Pastor and was on my way to your office."

Sharonda glanced at her father's closed door. "Me too. I mean … I planned to come find you after dropping this off." She held up the rally packet. "This won't take long." Did she imagine his cool demeanor? Once he heard her news, hopefully things would go back to the way they were.

"Please wait for me?"

Carl Ray walked further down the hall and leaned against the wall.

She knocked on her father's door.

"Come in," he called.

Sharonda paused and looked over her shoulder.

Looking comfortable in his golf shirt and khaki pants, Carl Ray took out his phone.

She blew out a long breath and entered.

Fifteen minutes later, Sharonda scurried from her father's work space.

Carl Ray looked up from his phone. His gaze never left her as she approached.

She smiled.

Would he take her hand? She yearned for the connection.

Carl Ray pocketed his cell and waved his hand forward for her to lead.

The muscles in her shoulders tightened. "I didn't mean for that to take so long."

"It worked out. I cleaned out my emails." His reticence filled the space around them.

She wished he'd say something else. Instead, silence hung between them all the way to her office. She passed through the entryway and spun around, looking to Carl Ray to direct her. Did she sit? Stand?

He paused outside the doorway.

Sharonda gathered the hem of her shirt between her thumb and first finger. "Are you coming in?"

He entered and immediately backed against the wall. "I'm leaving Longview."

Three words had never sounded so final. "You renewed your contract?" She managed to reach one of the wingback chairs and held on to the back for support.

"This morning." He pushed away from the wall.

"Did your decision have anything to do with Travis's announcement, or everything to do with New York City?" She dropped into the chair.

"Both." He sat on the edge of the other. "Sunday, I realized my usefulness here has ended. I learned *you* fight for the things you really want. I'm just not one of them."

She opened her mouth to counter his words.

He shook his head to silence her. "Your brother can do the job I've been performing. Isn't that why you had your father send for him?" He dropped his eyes toward the floor, but not before she glimpsed the sheen there.

"Yes, but that was before ... I was wrong. I didn't mean to hurt you."

"Don't worry. The rally will happen as planned. Only change, Travis will be leading the songs. We've gone over everything. Saw your mother in the Senior Center looking pretty much like her old self. All you need now is for your dad to become bishop, and it's a wrap. You'll have accomplished everything you set out to do. Everything you've fought for."

She stared into her lap. Did he think she'd used him? Hadn't she?

He took her hand. "I've apologized to you. Am I forgiven?"

Shouldn't she be the one to ask forgiveness? "Yes." She answered the spoken and unspoken question of marriage she hoped he'd ask again. Sharonda brought his hand to her face and leaned into his stiff palm. "I love you."

He pulled free. "Not enough to follow me. Not enough to fight for us."

"Is all of this because I didn't jump on the girl in your apartment and pull her hair out?"

At least he smiled. "I don't want you to do anything for me you don't want to."

"Now you know what I want to do or not?"

"I didn't come to argue."

Sharonda stood, faced him. "What *did* you come to do?"

He rose, towering over her. "To say goodbye."

She gripped the edge of her desk for balance. "When do you leave?" she whispered.

"I fly out today and report for work tomorrow. By the way, did you ever call Brice and end things?"

"I had made plans to ..." She lowered her gaze.

"Yeah, that's what I thought. I was warned. Call me a fool. I believed you loved me more."

She deserved his harsh words. "I wish you the best."

"This is where you're supposed to send me off into the sunset with a kiss, Scarlett." He closed the distance and lowered his head.

She couldn't look him in the eyes, so she linked her arms around his neck, squeezed her lids tight, and kissed him farewell.

Sharonda stared at her office door as it closed. Carl Ray had left for good. She plucked her phone out of her purse. It was time she started cleaning up her own house, even if she had to address one mess at a time.

She dialed Brice.

Chapter Seventeen

"Ten minutes." Sharonda directed from the stage. "Lunch has been sponsored. You'll find lemonade, tea, and coffee in the fellowship hall. Bathroom breaks are included. I suggest you use your time wisely." She hopped off the stage.

Sharonda walked the rows, clearing the path of candy wrappers, empty water bottles, and backpacks. Cleaning up behind the children had become a habit when thoughts of Carl Ray bombarded. Oh, the mistakes she'd made! Praying for him every night would have to suffice.

Janice stepped into the row and blocked Sharonda. "We have custodians. Better yet, instruct the kids to clean their trash at the end of practice. Cleaning now is a waste."

"And I keep finding you at church. Are you a new convert?"

"The entire family is tied up in your rally preparations. To see you guys, I have to come here. No one's home to eat my cooking." Janice pouted.

"I appreciate all you're doing to help around here. Thank you. But then again, you're lonely. Admit it."

"Got tired of the club scene. Guess I'm getting older." She stroked down Sharonda's arm. "Besides, someone needs to make sure you're taking breaks and eating. Your clothes are hanging off of you. The circles around your eyes have circles."

Sharonda pulled her shirt up on her shoulder. "Running nonstop doesn't leave much time to sit around eating." She stepped forward to pass, but Janice crossed her arms.

"Funny how the symptoms didn't exist until Carl Ray moved back to New York City. Are you ignoring his calls again?"

Sharonda sighed. "I wish."

"Nothing's stopping you from calling. Tell him you love him instead of crying through the night."

"Anything short of a brawl is worthless to him."

Janice scrunched her face. "What does that mean?"

"Leaving all I know to be his wife." Again, she tried to move past her sister.

Janice grabbed her shoulders. "Wait! What am I missing? Did you have the talk with Carl about your change of heart?"

"Mom and Dad still need me. My life is here." She looked at the crowd of kids rushing to the stage and waved. "They need me."

"From what I've seen this past month, you've merely existed, a shell of your old self." Janice put her hands on her hips. "Look at DeAnte and Patience. Their hormones are raging. They've been skulking in corners on every break, getting their feel on, and you're too busy moping to notice." She shook her head. "Listen up, stop worrying about everyone else's needs. Either convince Carl Ray to move here or you go to him, already. Last I checked, God didn't ask for your help." She walked away, catching up to the band members.

Janice made everything sound so simple.

Sharonda finished the row and collapsed into the last seat. *Patience.* She closed her eyes.

She'd forgotten all about addressing the rumors. The card and candy still sat in her office. Why hadn't she addressed the youth? Was her motivation to help Patience or herself? She served the children because it made *her* feel loved. Sharonda dropped her head into her hand, covering her face.

Oh God, forgive me. I've been so selfish. Here's my life, as messed up as it is. Do with it what You will.

"From the top," Travis instructed the reassembled band and performers.

Sharonda lifted her head to the sound of the children's voices.

Aaron rocked back and forth to the rhythm and sported a smile she'd never seen on the man's face. Maybe she should call Carl Ray. Tell him how Aaron and his wife now attended services together. He would be happy to learn Aaron had enrolled in an adult literacy class.

But would he want to hear it from *her*?

Emotion ballooned in her throat.

Sharonda watched Janice instruct the kids to take their places throughout the remainder of practice. When had her little sister become so responsible and so gifted with leading the young ones? New Hope volunteers and workers from the other churches joined her efforts on stage.

The kids recalled the words to the songs for the most part. Even the parts in Spanish, thanks to Casa de Oración's youth leaders. They'd have to work on getting the children to come in at the same time.

When the singers vacated the stage, children adorned in the costumes provided by Mobberly Baptist's youth department flooded in with activity. Their excitement to participate in a drama ministry—not available at their own church—filled the room.

Finally, Bethel Temple praise dancers moved across the stage and down into the audience, bringing the practice to a close. Sharonda jumped to her feet and applauded. "You do this in two weeks, and there won't be a dry eye in attendance. Keep up the good work, guys."

Boys' and girls' faces lit up brighter than the house lights.

"Pastor Nick Lawsen, please pray us out," Travis asked the visiting minister. After the amen, the auditorium roared to life with children horsing around, talking, and laughing.

"Bye, Ms. Peterson. You all right?"

"I'm fine." She waved to the group of girls from New Hope, not sure which one had actually spoken. "Monica, have you seen Patience?"

"No, ma'am."

"Thanks. Loved the effort y'all gave in practice." Sharonda continued to scan through the crowd for her mentee.

Most of the youth had vacated to the waiting area for pick-up. Maybe she'd missed her. Sharonda went out into the foyer and farther down the hallway leading into the classroom wing for a final search. She turned at the sound of voices and spotted a group of guys snickering outside a closed door.

They fell silent at her approach.

"What's going on?"

One fellow broke into a run and the others followed.

She peered through the classroom window. Her mouth gaped.

Two sets of eyes met hers. Both showed surprise. Sharonda looked away. She moved when the door opened and barely avoided colliding with DeAnte Adams who, built like a linebacker, rushed past her.

Sharonda entered, clasped her hands in front of her. "After you're finished, come to my office. We need to talk."

Patience stared at the floor, buttoning her shirt. "Please don't say anything to the Dowers." The girl never lifted her gaze.

"We'll discuss everything in my office." Sharonda closed the door on her way out.

She needed to sit and think through what she'd seen. What she'd say.

Oh, God. Sharonda sat at her desk. Had they gone all the way? Better yet, who was she to say anything? To have onlookers … she shook her head, not wanting to replay the image.

"You got something to say to me?" Patience stood stiff in the doorway.

"Come in and have a seat." Sharonda chewed the tip of her pen.

Patience sat, avoiding eye contact.

Sharonda approached the hurting young woman on the other side of her desk. She kneeled at the girl's feet and grabbed her hands until she looked at her. "First, let me start by saying, we're going to work through this together. We all make mistakes. I'm a living witness."

"I'm sorry." Patience broke and sobbed. She came out of the chair and into Sharonda's arms, making her careen backward.

Sharonda stroked Patience's back and arms, recalling how Carl Ray had soothed away her own fears when Mother had humiliated her in front of the dance team. "Cry it out." She rocked and held her close until her sobs quieted to a soft whimper. "Let's get your face dried, and I have a story to tell you."

They rose together.

Sharonda grabbed the Kleenex from the corner of her desk and handed the box to Patience.

Sharonda sat in the adjacent chair. "I remember a time when I was angry with God. Why didn't I get my brother's ability to sing? Why didn't I have my sister's looks and magnetic personality? Eating became my comfort."

She reached out and covered Patience's hand resting on the arm of the chair and leaned closer. "The kids picked on me. My loved ones disappointed me. And not thinking too much of myself, I sought comfort in the arms of a young boy—anything to feel beautiful, wanted, and in control of my life."

Patience turned her tear-streaked face to Sharonda. "But you *are* beautiful."

Sharonda smiled. "*You're* beautiful, too."

"I'm too tall."

"And I'm a big girl. We all come in different packages." Sharonda remembered Carl Ray's words. "God made you perfect. Are you calling Him a liar?"

"No, ma'am." That got a grin out of her. Patience's phone rang. She pulled it from her back pocket and silenced the ringtone. "I got to go. My ride's here."

Sharonda stood. "We better get you to the front for pick-up."

"Please don't tell the Dowers. They've been so nice, and I'm afraid this might make them get rid of me. I keep messing up."

"I'm afraid the kids will spread what happened. You don't want them to learn from anyone else, do you?"

"Can you tell them?" Patience gathered her backpack.

"I could, but I think they need to hear your heart. They love you. I'll be honored to be there by your side. Come on, let me walk you to the car."

Sharonda put her arm around the child's waist, escorted her to the last car waiting out front, and asked Mrs. Dowers for permission to come over later for a chat. They needed to develop an action plan before the next Sunday service. News like that would travel fast.

She walked back toward the youth building entrance.

"There you are." Janice met Sharonda entering through the double doors. "I've looked everywhere for you."

"I've been in my office talking with Patience. I just walked her to the car."

Janice frowned. "I sent Tasha to your office. She never came to tell me you were in there."

"Deacon Smith's daughter?" Janice's infamous informer. Skullduggery in the flesh.

"Yeah."

"I didn't see her. My door was open—" Sharonda covered her mouth.

Of all people, why had Janice sent her?

Chapter Eighteen

Sharonda added a small serving of her favorite creamed peas to her plate. "Janice, would you pass the Chow-chow?" Her mouth watered, anticipating the tangy cabbage mixed with the sweetness of the pale green vegetable.

Her sister placed the Mason jar of relish beside Sharonda. "Glad to see you're eating something besides rabbit food. Your meeting with the Dowers went well this morning?"

"It did." Sharonda spooned the condiment over her food as she lowered her voice, "They were very supportive of Patience. I still need to make Dad aware of what happened." She peered at her parents across the table. They'd leaned their heads together to converse. Janice nudged her with her elbow. "Do you plan to tell *all*?"

Mother looked their way.

Sharonda whispered, "We'll talk later."

Dad forked a baked chicken wing from the platter for Mother. Then, he turned to Sharonda and placed a chicken leg beside her roll.

She held up her hand when he tried to give her more. "No thanks. This is plenty."

"I've noticed your decreased appetite. Should I be concerned?" Dad offered the platter to Janice.

"Will I be hearing from Brice soon?" Mother unfolded her napkin.

"Probably not," Sharonda said.

"Revival season can be taxing. He'll get in touch."

"Brice hasn't visited in months, Mother. I suggested we continue our relationship as friends. He seemed very pleased to retract his marriage offer."

Mother's eyes widened. "You did what? You *must* be on your cycle? Nothing else would explain such a ridiculous action. Sharonda, you should've discussed this with me first." The real Marianne Peterson finally put in an appearance.

"I don't love him," Sharonda slipped out a little above a whisper.

"Our children are grown. Our daughter has made an adult decision that she will have to live with." Dad cut into his chicken breast.

"I hope you understand what you've done. You aren't getting younger, and with your condition ..." Mother huffed. "There goes my hopes of becoming a grandmother, but I'll support whatever makes *you* happy. Within reason." She adjusted the silverware next to her plate.

Sharonda motioned toward her siblings. "You have two more children."

Janice shook her head. "Not me. I don't even want kids."

"I'll pass," Travis said.

Mother waved her hand between them. "By the time they get their lives together, I may be in a convalescent home."

"Hold up. According to Derrick, Carl Ray arranged a special date in New York to present *you* with an engagement ring." Her brother drenched his salad with dressing.

Sharonda coughed, spraying peas over the table.

"Did I speak out of turn?" Travis picked the uninvited vegetables from his plate.

Mother held her fork in midair. "*What?*"

"Don't upset yourself, Marianne." Dad patted her hand. "I'm sure there's an explanation why the church drummer knows my daughter has accepted a ring I know nothing about." He raised his brow toward Sharonda.

A ring? Sharonda knocked the chair over as she stood. "Sorry." She rushed from the table.

"Come back here, young lady," Mother said.

She kept walking. "I can't do this anymore." She forced the words out.

"Let her go," Dad said.

Sharonda hurried to her room and burrowed beneath the covers. "My life is in Your hands." She wasn't sure if she offered a prayer or asked for help, but an awareness of God's presence filled her until nothing mattered. Flipping on her side, she propped a pillow between her knees and slept.

"Sharonda."

Someone shook her. She peered through slits in her eyes, Mother sat on the edge of the mattress beside her. Dad occupied a chair close by, while Janice looked at her from the other twin bed.

Uh-oh. The last time they'd met like this, Dad confronted Travis about the baby rumors. She sat up and pushed back against her pillows.

Janice cleared her throat. "I'm here as a support."

Travis poked his head in the doorway. "What happened in New York? Did you say no?"

Dad frowned as he faced Travis.

Her brother held up both hands. "I know. 'Shut up, Travis.' I'm leaving. Janice, fill me in later."

She crossed her arms.

"Or not." He closed the door.

Sharonda pulled the comforter up to her neck. "Carl Ray never presented me with a ring."

Dad angled toward her. "Would you please fill us in on what's going on?"

"Over a month ago, Carl Ray took me to New York City for the day." Unable to look at her parents, Sharonda repositioned a pillow.

"Don't worry, Mother, I went with them." Janice scooted to the edge of her bed.

Travis came inside and leaned against the wall. "Hard to listen through a closed door. Just one question, then you won't know I'm here. Why New York?"

Sharonda sighed. "Carl Ray had a meeting with his agent and planned to take me out on the town afterward. He'd already proposed." Underneath her father's iron gaze, Sharonda stammered. "I asked him to wait to speak to you, Dad. *My* decision, not his."

"I went shopping," Janice said.

"He was gone a long time, and I didn't want to go out into the city. That place is way too active."

Her mother threw her hand up. "Young lady, get to the point."

"I fell asleep in Carl Ray's apartment."

Mother gasped.

"I was *alone*. Like I said, he was gone. The day didn't go according to his plans. While I was in another room, a fan broke into the apartment. I heard Carl Ray yell. That's when I found both of them in the front living area. He kicked the person out." The woman's slim lines and curves resurfaced in Sharonda's thoughts. She pinched the bridge of her nose and tried to blink the image away.

"I knew anything more than friendship between us couldn't work." She lifted her chin. "Dad, you said so yourself. I'm not his type. Some real beauties live in that city."

"*You're* beautiful." The tenderness in Mother's voice caused Sharonda to tense.

"But?"

Mother furrowed her brow.

"I'd be prettier if I lost weight. Isn't that what you were about to say?"

"I only wanted to motivate you to be healthier. It was never my intention to hurt you." Mother lowered her eyes.

"But you did." She couldn't keep the years of pain from sounding in her voice.

"I'm ... I'm sorry." Mother covered Sharonda's hand with hers.

She gripped her mother's long fingers, one of the few physical traits they shared, and accepted the most heartfelt apology she'd ever received. "Do you know what Carl Ray said when I tried to end the engagement?" She sniffled.

Mother's gaze remained on their joined hands. "Enlighten us."

Janice handed them both a tissue.

"Big decisions shouldn't be made on an empty stomach. Then he treated me to the best pizza I've ever eaten." Sharonda laughed.

Dad stood and draped his arm across Mother's shoulders. "Sounds like Carl Ray is a wise young man."

"Where's the ring?" Travis reminded everyone of his presence.

Sharonda shrugged. "I don't know."

"Would the ring have changed things?" Mother said.

"I don't think so. His world is so different from mine. Here, I have my work. I know what to do."

"If that were true, why are you hiding in here?"

Sharonda sighed. Oh, how she wished her sister would hush.

"That's enough. You are in no position to question your sister. We're done here." Mother released her hand with an assuring pat and stood.

"All right, everybody, you heard your mother. Out," Dad said.

"There's one more thing. We may have a problem at the church." Sharonda glanced between her parents.

Dad nodded. "Sounds serious. Why don't we talk in my office? There, people can't stand behind doors and listen."

"That's my cue." Travis darted from the room.

꿈

A week later, Sharonda sat before the church's disciplinary board waiting for the members to determine her future. Not only had her conversation with Patience been overheard, but recorded and viewed on social media.

"Who were you talking to in your office? Or must we rely on the scandalous video?" Deacon Smith showed himself to be the undercover bully she'd long suspected hid beneath his holy title and church works.

Sharonda remained silent.

Deacon Smith scoffed and motioned to the board member holding the remote. "Play the video. Looks like Sister Peterson is choosing not to answer. After this, you'll see why I'm petitioning to hire a new youth director."

She'd given her life to this ministry and everything came down to a vote. Sharonda sat tall in her seat, her father at the head of the conference table with the other board members, and her mother at her side.

The recording projected onto the pull-down screen. Her office's wingback chair obscured Patience's face in the video and muffled enough of the conversation to conceal the girl's identity. Sharonda relaxed her shoulders. But her voice came through clear as she shared with Patience how she'd sought comfort in the arms of a young boy. She stared straight ahead and her chest ached with remorse.

Deacon Smith motioned to pause the video and spun around in his chair. "I'll ask you one more time, who were you talking to? We can't have the young people thinking they can come into the house of the Lord with their filthiness and there not be any consequences. Or would you have the church teaching them it's okay to indulge sins of the flesh so they can 'feel beautiful, and in control of their life?'"

"You're taking her words out of context, Deacon," Mother said.

Why couldn't the video portray Sharonda's remorse? Or the crippling hurt embedded deep inside Patience's heart?

"Sister Peterson, am I to assume by your continued silence there's more to the story? Rumor has it you're covering for the child because you had a few escapades of your own. We heard how Mr. Everheart frequented the youth building."

Mother pressed her hand against Sharonda's leg when she tried to stand.

Dad stood. "You are out of line." He spoke with authority.

Several nodded and a few mumbled their support.

"This church has never entertained rumors. You will not introduce them into our proceedings now. Do I make myself clear?"

Deacon Smith narrowed his eyes. "Yes, you've made it clear that you are willing to turn your back on your children's sin."

"We've viewed the *presented evidence*." Harold Newsome, the oldest member on the board, took over. "Sister Peterson, do you have anything to say in your defense before we ask you to step out while we put the matter up for a vote?"

Sharonda pushed away from the table and stood. "I know it looks bad, especially with the limited footage of our conversation. My only intentions were to share my testimony with a hurting young lady. Remind her how we all make mistakes, therefore our need of the Savior." She gazed into the eyes of the remaining men still seated around the table. "Whatever the outcome, whether I'm youth director or not, please make sure the Rally continues. The young people have worked so hard." She headed for the door. She wouldn't look back.

Outside the conference room, Sharonda dropped into the leather chairs and waited.

Chapter Nineteen

Carl pulled his leading lady, Kristy, into his arms with more force than he'd intended and looked into her eyes. They weren't as deep as the script called for but sang love's promise to be there.

What was his problem? Women wanted him, but the ones he loved walked out of his life. If only he could convince his heart to stop hoping.

As he finished the song, Kristy leaned into his chest and planted what should have been a stage kiss fully on his mouth.

In his mind, he and Sharonda were in her office, saying good-bye again. Unlike now, he'd put everything into that kiss, begging her to ask him to stay.

"Cut," Chad yelled through the megaphone.

Carl broke contact, causing Kristy to stumble. "Sorry." He steadied her before walking away.

"Good job, everybody. Everhart?" Chad called.

Carl turned toward the director.

"Eat some lunch and come back a changed man. This is the part in the play where you sell tickets. You're holding a beautiful woman in your arms. Act like it."

He saluted him and left the stage.

Outside his dressing room, Kristy stood with other female cast members. "Carl? We have reservations. Join us?" She glanced at her friends before making eye contact with him.

He worked to give his co-star a smile. "Thanks, but no." Carl ignored the disappointed sighs as he entered his dressing room. He locked the door behind him and dropped into the chair. Reaching beneath the vanity and inside his duffle, Carl retrieved the gray pillowcase. He clutched the material and took a deep breath. Sharonda's signature warm vanilla and berries scent was long gone and only remained as a faded memory after a couple months in his bag.

Much like his life, his apartment had lost its appeal since she'd gone. The city's view now dimmed in comparison to the way her eyes lit when she'd stood mirrored in its reflection.

Maybe he should've shown her the ring.

He lifted his gaze to the ceiling. "Didn't I obey and go home? I apologized. I proposed. What else would You have me do?"

Silence.

Carl flung the pillowcase into the waste basket. Bumping the table with his knee, his framed glamor shot slid down the wall. Shattered glass covered the vanity. What was left in his life to shatter? He shook his head. "Who am I that You should answer me?"

Only what you do for Christ will last.

Carl rubbed the stubbles on his jaw. His trip to his hometown hadn't been about him, had it?

I fight your battles.

God spared his life and he complained. *Forgive me, Lord.*

Carl retrieved the pillowcase and raked the shards into the trash. He reclined in his chair and set his phone to blast his worship play list, his first step to getting in the right frame of mind.

After lunch, Carl crossed the stage. He grinned at the director and nodded greetings to his fellow cast members.

"Let's take it from the top of the third scene. Mr. Everhart, I hope you took advantage of the break. We need some energy from you. We're paying you a lot of money."

"I'm ready."

Hours later, Carl walked through the door of his apartment building, humming the play's closing number. He slowed to acknowledge the concierge. "Terry, how's the family?"

He smiled so brightly it outshone the brass buttons decorating his uniform. "Wonderful. Baby girl is growing fast. The wife has recovered and she's working out to tackle the stubborn 'baby fat' as she calls it."

Carl lowered his voice. "Anything that doesn't fit inside the hand, running over, is a blessing in my book."

He remembered going home, knowing Sharonda was there and remembered how it felt to hold her in his arms. He remembered everything all too well. His heart ached. "You're blessed beyond measure. Enjoy it, man." Carl took a step toward the elevator.

"Mr. Everhart. You have a guest waiting for you in the café, sir."

"Alexis? Short lady in a red jacket, company emblem on the right?" Carl glanced at the designated spot in front of the coffee shop. "She's my new agent."

"An older woman. Been here since this morning. Maybe a couple hours after you left for the theater."

He furrowed his brow. "She didn't give you a name?"

Terry tipped his head. "Here she comes now."

Marianne Peterson walked toward him. The pink suit, coiffed hair, and block-heeled shoes marked her as a churchgoing woman even for the folks who didn't attend on a regular basis.

Carl stood straighter. Her stately posture had that kind of effect on him. "First Lady, I mean no disrespect when I say this, but what are you doing here?" He looked toward the coffee shop. "Did Pastor come with you?"

"I'm intentionally alone. Can we go somewhere and talk? I have to fly out today. The Uber people will be here in another hour to drive me to the airport."

"Something wrong?"

Lady Peterson patted his arm. "I'd rather not speak here."

"Let's go to my apartment. Have you eaten? I can order take-out."

"Thank you. My daughter tells me the pizza here is wonderful." She grinned.

Carl frowned. How much had Sharonda shared about their trip? He reached in his pocket for his money clip and handed Terry enough bills to cover the tab and a generous tip. "One stuffed meat-lovers and two big salads." He extracted another bill. "This should be enough to get baby girl something from her uncle Carl."

"Thank you."

The elevator dinged open.

"You better hurry, sir."

Once they reached his apartment, Carl motioned for Lady Peterson to enter ahead of him.

"A nice place you have here. A far cry from the life we live in Longview." She faced him and crossed her arms. "*You* even look different."

He ran a hand down the front of his shirt. "I admit things are different here, but I'm the same Carl Ray."

"Are you?" She raised a perfectly arched brow. "The young man I witnessed praying at the altar with his fellow musicians had a certain excitement about him. That same man dared stand up to me in my daughter's office. Determination put swagger in his steps." She tisked. "A changed man, I'd say. That's the man I've come to apologize to. The same man I'm counting on to finish what he started. Without my interference."

Did she know about the engagement? *Breathe.*

"Lady Peterson, please, have a seat."

"If you don't mind, I'll walk. I've sat more than I want to today." She moved to the window and looked out over the city. "Why did you return to Longview? Your family was out of the country. You could've completed your recovery here."

"Something happened on that hospital bed. I had too many unanswered questions."

When she continued to stare out of the window, he walked into the kitchen and called to her. "Would you like something to drink? I have water and juice."

"Water would be nice."

Carl returned, bottle in hand. "I could pour this in a glass if you prefer."

158

Lady Peterson accepted the drink and held his gaze. "Why did you leave New Hope?"

He stepped back. "When did you say you had to return?"

She smiled. "I guess I deserved that. I'm told my direct approach can be offensive at times."

Carl downed half of his bottle and wiped his mouth with the back of his hand. "To answer your question, Travis returned. Everything I'd come home to do had been done."

"*You* were to headline at the youth rally. Are you planning to fly in and perform?"

"I thought Travis would."

"My son's being there has nothing to do with *your* assignment."

"I ..." He peered out the window and thought about the last Peterson who'd stood next to him in the same spot. "You're right."

"I believe if Sharonda had agreed to marry you, you'd still be in Longview."

Carl opened his mouth to speak just as the doorbell sounded. "Dinner."

"Your restroom?"

He pointed toward the hall, then answered the door.

Mother Peterson strolled into the kitchen soon after he'd set the table. "Smells great."

"Would you like for me to pray? I'm sure you're as hungry as I am."

"We can eat after you tell me why you've given up on my daughter. We both know the real reason you returned to Longview."

Had he given up?

"I'd hate for the food to get cold," she chided.

Chapter Twenty

Sharonda slid a bowl of buttered popcorn onto the coffee table, within reach of Janice, Travis, and Derrick. "Guys, thank you for coming." She sat next to her brother on the sectional.

"No problem," Derrick said.

"I'm sure you've heard by now that I've been officially suspended of all church duties for the next six months. If Deacon Smith had gotten his way, I'd be permanently removed as youth director. Thank God the church doesn't rely on the suggestion of one board member." She sniffed.

Janice squeezed her hand.

She smiled at her sister. "However, the Rally is a go if I can prove to the board there's leadership in place."

Travis grabbed the popcorn. "Reschedule the date until you are reinstated. Problem solved."

"No, it's not. This event involves other churches. It's not fair to change the schedule because of one person. The event needs to proceed as planned, without me."

"But you didn't do anything wrong," Janice cut in. "Well, not recently. Shouldn't there be a statute of limitations or something?"

Sharonda shook her head. "It's not meant as penance. I need this opportunity to strengthen my relationship with God. The date on which it happened doesn't matter. I've rationalized my behavior for too long."

Travis put his arm around her shoulders. "We've all made mistakes. Isn't that what you were saying to Patience?"

Sharonda sighed. "I don't have to guess if you saw the video."

"I had to see what the buzz was about. Two, I never would've believed it was you. You've always lived by the Book."

Her throat tightened with emotion. "That's what I hoped everyone would believe. I almost convinced myself. A pretender. But no more."

Travis brushed circles on her arm. "Don't get me wrong, sis, I'm not putting you down. Your reaction to everything has made me feel the need to reexamine my own life. You seem happier. Confident. I want what you've found."

Sharonda grabbed a tissue from the end table. "Sorry, guys. Might as well keep this close." She placed the box in her lap. "I'm not permitted to act in any leadership roles. That's where you all come in. Derrick, you've worked with Carl Ray and me from the beginning. I need you to step up and take my place."

"Why not someone from the Youth department?" Derrick scooped a handful of popcorn.

"You understand the vision Carl Ray and I had for this event. You saw how we worked with the teens, held meetings, and made phone calls to the leaders from the different ministries.

"You'll have plenty of help." Sharonda nodded toward Janice. "My sister has agreed to assist you. Any errands you need done, she's your girl."

The drummer folded his arms and stared at her.

"Unless you have someone else in mind?"

He sighed and shook his head.

"Good. I need this event to emphasize our attempt to love our neighbors. Can I count on you to carry the torch in our absence?"

Travis reached for the bowl. "Our? Like you and Carl are still a couple?"

"Shut up, Travis," Janice scolded.

"I'm glad to help in any way you need me," Derrick said.

"Are you all saying yes?" Sharonda steepled her fingers.

They all nodded.

"Great."

Derrick turned to Janice. "Are you sure you'll have time to work with me? If I remember correctly, you keep a busy schedule."

Janice ran her finger over the rim of her glass. "I said I'd help."

Derrick passed her his cell. "I need your information."

"Travis, how far are you from learning the lead parts to the songs?" Sharonda said.

"I'm having to change some things to fit my lower range. I'm no Carl Ray, but I'll do my best."

Sharonda nodded. "I'm grateful for what you *all* are doing. Never would've guessed we'd be collaborating on a project together."

"We're family," Janice piped in.

"I second that," Travis said.

Sharonda stretched her hand out. "Youth rally on three."

Others piled their hands on top of hers. United, they counted and said, "Youth Rally!"

If only Carl Ray were here to share in the moment he'd helped create.

❧

Sharonda pumped her arms to keep up with Patience's pace through the mall. "How was school this week?"

"It's getting better." Patience adjusted her damp headband. "How is it that the same boys who put me on blast for making out in the classroom are applauding DeAnte? I'm a slut and he's the man. How can that be?"

"I don't know. That's how it's been as far back as I can remember." Sharonda slowed and took a sip of water. "What's the status of your relationship with him?"

"He avoided me when we went back to school." She huffed. "He didn't love me. The counselor at We Grow Up says I have to first learn to love myself to know what it looks like."

"That's a lesson I'm working on right along with you. God was deliberate when creating me."

Patience pretended to shoot a basket. "Glad He didn't create me for basketball. That takes a coordination I don't have, tall or not."

163

Sharonda laughed. "I know. What if you were meant to be a genetic carrier for the child you'll have one day? Someone has to give birth to the next NBA star."

"Or WNBA." Patience nodded.

"Did you hear the rally is a go?"

"I did." She picked up the pace.

When Patience didn't say more, Sharonda added. "Do you plan to participate?"

"Probably not."

"If your decision has anything to do with a group of young men, I believe it's best to face your nay-sayers. Running empowers them. Face them and your past loses its power over you."

"I hear you, but I'm not sure I can. Especially since you won't be there."

"I'll be in the audience on performance day, but you don't need me." Sharonda looped arms with Patience and slowed her stride. "This is your chance to be an example to some other young lady. They need to know a mistake is not the end of the world. We overcome with God's help. You have to believe it first."

Patience stopped and faced Sharonda. "Every day at school, I hear some female make a comment about how stupid I am. How I'm trash. Not exactly role model material."

"What are you saying about yourself? You are fearfully and wonderfully made. Tell you what, you say it to me and I'll say it to you until we believe it. Okay?"

Patience gave Sharonda a sweaty hug. "I love you, Ms. P. Thanks for not giving up on me."

"I expect to see you at the rally. Wear a pair of heels. Embrace the package God gave you. Tall *is* beautiful."

❧

Sharonda pulled the last section of her hair through the flat iron.

Janice poked her head into the bathroom. "Why all the extra care with your hair? It's a youth rally, not Sunday service."

"Did Patience make it to practice?" Sharonda moved past her sister, grabbed the gold-trimmed hat from the closet, and placed the box on the bed beside her outfit. She nodded, satisfied with her selections.

"I see you've been shopping without me." Janice lifted the garment and touched the lining. "Is this a custom or a ready-made?"

Sharonda snatched her clothes from her sister and stepped inside the off-white swing dress. She presented her exposed back to Janice.

"I'm your lady's maid now?" Janice zipped. "Is it your intent to arrive early? At this rate, you'll be at the rally two hours before the kids."

"I have a stop to make."

"Who are you meeting?" Janice crossed her arms.

Sharonda walked back to the bathroom to check her reflection in the mirror. "You never told me if Patience made it to practice."

"Why are you avoiding my questions? Is it Carl Ray?"

"If you must know, I've decided to fight for the things I want." Sharonda straightened her hat.

"Dressed like that?" Janice smirked. "You're not *fighting* fair. He won't be able to resist. I'm so proud of you."

"Does Derrick know you've got a thing for him?" Sharonda returned the smirk.

"I'll take these to the car for you." Janice grabbed the hat box and Sharonda's Bible. She hurried from the room.

Sharonda laughed and called after her sister. "Who's running now? Trust me, it's better to face your fears head on."

No quick comeback? Or fly words? Her footsteps receded and the front door opened and closed. Would she ever understand that sister of hers?

Sharonda finished getting ready. Once she pulled out onto the street, she sang with the radio, "V-I-C-T-O-R-Y."

She prayed as she drove through town. Finding a vacant spot, she killed the engine and walked to the passenger side to get her hat.

Sharonda approached the front door, and knocked as if she'd gloved up to box.

"Coming! Now stop hitting my door befo' I call the police."

Sharonda forced her shoulders back and flipped the brim of her hat. "It's me, Grandma."

Chapter Twenty-One

Carl peered out the window, his mood captured in the darkness of the city's angry sky. Raindrop veins pulsed along the pane. The intercom buzzed four times before he wandered into the kitchen and pushed the call button.

"Do you have time to visit with your god-niece?" Terry's voice bellowed through the speakers.

The baby's coos filtered into the silence of his apartment.

He viewed the room's unkempt conditions. "Sure, man, I'll come right down."

"It's my lunch break and I have the wife with me. We could come up."

Carl gripped the side of his neck. "Okay." He scrambled to clear take-out boxes from the countertops and dumped them into the stainless-steel trash receptacle. From the living room furniture, he heaped two days' worth of piled clothes into his arms and carried them to the washer down the hall. Back in the kitchen, he transferred the few real dishes he owned from the sink into the dishwasher as the doorbell chimed. Carl blotted moisture from his brow and headed for the entrance. "Welcome."

Terry stood with his wife tucked under his arm, her hands resting on a yellow stroller.

The picture-perfect family, envy taunted. "Come on in," Carl said.

The couple wheeled the baby inside. "Raven, meet Uncle Carl." Terry chuckled. "This is who sent the money for Ella."

A smile dimpled Raven's round cheeks. "I've already started a penny bank for the baby." She leaned into her husband's side.

He caressed her shoulder. "The man won't bite, sweet pea. We're friends." He addressed Carl. "My wife's a bit celebrity-shy. She comes from a little hick town in Ore City, Texas. You can be a little intimidating for her kind." He winked.

She slapped his arm, but her smile remained.

"I know the place. I was born and raised in Longview. How did you guys meet?" Carl said.

Raven looked at her husband, but he shrugged and laughed. She nibbled her bottom lip and reached inside the stroller to comfort the squirming babe. "The Internet," she answered.

Terry nodded. "I knew she was the one. Took me a long time to convince her to move here and marry me, though. Even longer to persuade her parents. They soon realized I wasn't going away."

She gazed up at her husband all dreamy-eyed as if he'd spun the world on its axis.

Carl cleared his throat.

Terry pressed a kiss to Raven's forehead. "Man, I don't know why she puts up with me. I can't wait to treat this woman to the life she deserves." He lifted the baby from the stroller. "Right now, I work two jobs and tackle online courses, so Raven can stay home and care for Ella. We live with my auntie so I can help take care of her place, while I save up for one of our own. It helps that she's out of town working more than she's home. Gave us some time to adjust to our new addition." Terry held the baby out to Carl.

Baby freshness engulfed him as Terry laid the child in his arms. He adjusted Carl's hands to better secure the wiggling bundle. She had a head full of tight black curls. Carl nuzzled the downy rolls at her neck.

The baby whimpered.

Did she sense his nervousness? "You may want to take her. I'm not good with handling delicate packages," Carl said.

"Don't give up so fast. She'll adjust." Terry helped Carl bring the baby to the center of his chest and guided him to make circles on her back.

He walked the floor, bouncing Ella. As he hummed, the baby's breathing slowed and the wiggles left her body. She snuggled into the crook of his neck. Carl hugged her softness.

"Aren't you glad I made you hold on a little longer? Ain't nothing like it, man," Terry said.

What if he'd held onto Sharonda a little longer, reassured her fears? Would things be different?

"Ella likes to hear a heartbeat. Her momma taught me that trick."

"There you go. Be patient with your Uncle Carl. We're learning together." He peered down into her sleeping face. "She's perfect. Forgive my manners. Please, make yourselves comfortable. Sit wherever you like."

Terry shook his head. "Can't stay. My sister is downstairs waiting on Raven. Maneuvering the city is still a challenge for her. But she didn't let that stop her today." Terry puffed his chest out. "The wife wanted to surprise me. You did good, babe. Made my day." He stroked her jaw.

Lightening streaked the sky, followed by a rumble, then a boom.

The baby startled. Carl rubbed her back as he rocked and stole glances at her parents.

That could've been me and Sharonda.

Could've, should've, would've—none of that would make him and Sharonda a reality. His mind drifted to when First Lady Peterson sat across from him at his table. She'd known the root of why he returned to Longview and came all the way to the Big Apple to confront him. He railed at Sharonda for not fighting for their relationship. Had he?

≈

Sharonda spoke close to her grandmother's ear. "I'm so glad you came with me."

"Did I have a choice?" First Lady Dorothy Haynes lifted her chin higher as they walked into the auditorium for the rally. "You were right. In the face of rumors, the church needs to see that the first family is united."

She took a deep breath and—matching the matriarch's erect stride—met the gazes of all who nodded or waved a greeting. If she thought her mother's First Lady bearings were regal, Grandma's demeanor trumped them.

An older woman—smothered in rhinestones—hesitated as she approached. She took a second look and dipped her head toward Grandma.

"Praise the Lord, dear." Grandma extended a gloved hand.

The older woman clasped her fingers and smiled. She made a hasty retreat.

"Is she supposed to be here?" came a faceless whisper.

Fight or flight? Sharonda froze and looked straight ahead.

"That's the youth director. Why wouldn't she be here?"

"Heard her own daddy relieved her of her own duties."

"Come, dear." Grandma tugged Sharonda's arm.

Her feet hesitated to obey. *I'm not here for anyone but Patience and the young people in the program.*

Grandma glanced her way and lifted her head high again as if to model what she should be doing in the face of her accusers.

Sharonda adjusted her hat and followed her grandma's example. They walked toward the front seating reserved for her parents. She smiled and gestured for Grandma to enter the row, placing her next to her daughter.

Mother turned toward them and covered her unmistakable gasp with a gloved hand.

Grandma leaned close to Sharonda. "It's sad my presence brings out such surprise, but that's my fault. I plan to rectify that." Her so-called whisper was loud enough for anyone nearby to hear. She eased down into the tight space and tilted her head toward Mother. "Sometimes, it takes the younger generation to remind us what's important."

"I'm so glad you came," Mother said, a hitch in her voice.

Grandma patted her hands.

Sharonda left her mother and grandmother and made her way to the corner of the row behind them. She didn't want her hat to block anyone's view. Sharonda caught glimpses of her sister scurrying back and forth, obviously making last-minute runs before the curtains opened.

Dad walked out on the stage. "Welcome, everyone," his voice boomed, silencing the audience. The Channel 30 News crew directed their camera lights on him as he recited the Occasion listed in the bulletin. "Our mission is for the church bodies to be a community, loving in unity."

Pastors and church leadership from participating ministries in the Longview area walked onto the stage and linked hands, Dad being the center that linked them together.

In unison, the audience stood and did as their leaders before them.

Sharonda reached inside her clutch bag for a tissue.

"Father, humbly we come before You in need of your forgiving power. We as a people, as a family, as a community have failed to love as you commanded ..." Dad's words rang clear and bold. When he finished, he passed the microphone to other leaders who added their prayers. The lights dimmed in the auditorium, the curtains opened, and the show started.

By the third act, Sharonda had laughed so hard her sides hurt. A praise dancer lost a flag mid-leap, almost hitting a gentleman in the first row. Someone in the wings fed the skit performers missed lines, making the comedy act even funnier. The audience sobered as soon as the little fifth grader belted out a rendition of "Amazing Grace," sure to move the hearts of all present.

Sharonda leaned forward for a better view of her family. Dad handed Grandma his handkerchief, and she dabbed the corners of her eyes. He smiled down at her.

Patience wore a pair of heels causing her to tower over her schoolmates as she recited a work by the great poet Maya Angelou. One of her own words best described the youth rally. Phenomenal.

The Lobos' marching band closed with "We Are One" by The City Harmonic. Dancers in coordinating white bodysuits painted the stage with flags and streamers in a multitude of color. Every child in the program left their positions on aluminum platforms and became the choir. They'd part like the Red Sea to reveal the featured singer.

Sharonda waited for her brother to appear in the white tux. Where Travis's voice should have taken the lead, Carl Ray's filled the auditorium.

171

He wasn't in New York, but here in Longview, at New Hope Church. People jumped to their feet.

Gravity worked like a suction, trapping her where she sat.

Carl Ray closed his eyes and sang the song's convicting words as the young people joined in one accord.

When he sang, "every tongue and tribe in Jesus crucified," dancers expertly manipulated crimson fabric to flood the scenery. The crowd "ooohed" and "ahhhhed." The drum cadence rumbled through her chest. Then, the red converted back into the kaleidoscope of colors it'd once been.

When the performers and Carl Ray linked hands, so did the crowd. Composed of different races, genders, status, and denomination, they exhibited the message of the evening. To respect. To love. To unite.

At least she felt those things when her neighbor extended a hand and offered a smile.

Sharonda stood. Goosebumps lifted on her arms when she found Carl Ray looking in her direction.

Just tell him you love him, Janice's advice resurfaced. Would he give her another chance?

It's too late.

Fight! Sharonda silenced the doubt.

                        ≈

Carl kept his focus on Sharonda once he'd found her in the audience. Her gold-trimmed hat shimmered beneath the auditorium lights. As soon as he left the height of the stage, he lost his view of her. Smiles, handshakes, and the occasional pose for a picture with a kid and the parents had never seemed so tedious. While making small talk with a gentleman and his son, Carl spotted his agent. The red jacket made it easy to locate Alexis. He signaled for her help.

"Excuse me." Carl handed the autographed program back to the teenager. He took a step, but the dad blocked him.

"Have you considered hosting an acting camp for kids?" The overzealous man continued with the conversation Carl Ray thought he'd ended.

Alexis touched his arm. "Mr. Everhart? You have to wrap things up. Your plane leaves in two hours." She turned to the man and the youth. "I'm sure you understand his obligation to meet with as many fans as possible."

The father nodded. His puppy-dog gaze lingered on Alexis.

Carl glanced at his hand and saw no ring. He couldn't blame the dad for appreciating God's creation. His agent was a beautiful woman.

"Sure. I understand. Thanks for the autograph, Mr. Everhart." He moved away with his son and melted into the crowd.

Carl chuckled. Smooth and efficient. He bowed with a fancy roll of his hand, praising her work. Hiring her had been one of his better decisions.

He searched the crowd again. The gold of Sharonda's hat drew his attention. She ducked into a row.

Carl Ray frowned. Was she moving closer or further away? Maybe returning had been a mistake. Rejection might be a monster, but *public* rejection was a beast.

Chapter Twenty-Two

The cast bowed as the curtains closed.

Sharonda clapped so hard her hands stung. She couldn't decide who she was more proud of. Her dad for challenging them to reach the community? Patience? Or Carl Ray?

Cast members descended the stairs and mingled with the audience. Carl Ray appeared to be the main attraction with cell phones flashing around him as people squeezed close to capture selfies. A young man handed Carl Ray a marker and he scribbled across a kid's t-shirt.

Sharonda tiptoed and leaned sideways, struggling to keep him in her sights. So close, but so far removed from the place she'd once occupied in his life.

Remember, he wanted to marry you.

She quickened her steps, ramming into the woman ahead of her. "Sorry, I didn't see you stop."

The mother secured the whining toddler in her arms. "No problem." She adjusted a pink bag at her shoulder and whispered into the child's ear.

Sharonda tapped her foot, keeping an eye on Carl Ray. She hoped the man and boy would detain him long enough for her to …

Do what?

The lady in front of her stepped into the aisle and moved with the current of people headed in the direction of the stage.

Sharonda stopped at the end of the row. Who was she kidding? Carl Ray had gone on with his life, but why was he here? The person behind bumped her into the aisle.

175

"Ms. Peterson." Patience grabbed her arm and pulled her into the row behind the one she'd vacated.

Patience giggled. "You're no better in heels than I am. I've been a human machine, mowing people down all evening."

Sharonda adjusted her hat. "I'm so proud of you! The platform heels were a smart choice. You look good in yellow."

"Thank you, Ms. P. I want you to meet my friend, Marissa. She attends Mobberly church. Is it okay to invite her to join our workouts?"

Patience stood tall, but her friend stretched wide and wore thick glasses.

Thank you, Lord. You provided a confidant for Patience. One prayer answered.

Sharonda focused on the front. An attractive woman in a red jacket drew close to Carl Ray. "I'd love for you to join us, but I'll need to talk with your parents or a guardian first." She rose up on tiptoe to keep a clear vision of the two. Who was she? Had Carl Ray replaced her that quickly?

The girls snickered.

Sharonda looked from one to the other. "I'm sorry, did you say something?"

"Somebody's distracted," Patience sassed. She spoke to Marissa. "When Mr. Everhart worked here as our minister of music, he visited Ms. P. on the regular. Don't let us hold you up."

"Sorry, girls. We could plan to—"

Patience leaned down for a quick hug. "No. Go. We're out of here." She and her friend darted into the crowd, juvenile shrieks trailing their departure.

Surrounded by a new group of people, Carl Ray hadn't moved. Nor had the woman in red.

Sharonda pulled at her dress. Even with her new waistline, she could never compete with the petite woman and manageable hips.

Sharonda dug her nails into her palms. What kind of role model would she be to the young ladies, making comparisons and tearing herself down?

176

I am who You say I am.

Sharonda stepped into the aisle again. Baby steps, but she moved forward.

"Lift your head, child, 'fore you run into somebody," Grandmother scolded.

"Grandma. I was—"

"Going to escort me up front to meet *The* Carl Everhart. I hear you have a few connections." She looped her arm through Sharonda's and pulled her forward. "Why didn't you tell me the man eats dinner with you and the family when he's in town? Let's invite him over. And I need his autograph." Grandmother handed her a pen and pad.

"Who told you he comes to dinner?" Sharonda looked back. Her mother waved.

"I love you, Grandma." She matched the older woman's regal posture. "This is why I need you to get well."

"Sad you had to remind your old grandma she still has responsibilities. Also, your mother needs some grandbabies to remind her of *her* age." She laughed.

Laughter, a sound she hoped would return to her family. *All* of her family. Sharonda smiled and walked toward Carl Ray.

He'd knelt beside a young girl to pose for a picture.

When the child walked away, Carl Ray stood. He held her gaze for a brief moment then looked away before Sharonda could respond to the mixed emotions she read on his face.

Fight or flight. Had she chosen the wrong one?

❦

The house lights bounced off the gold of Sharonda's hat as she approached with a notepad that carried one word on the cover. Autographs.

He heaved a sigh and looked away. After all they'd been through, she approached him as a fan? She only wanted his signature when he'd offered her his heart?

177

Alexis invaded his peripheral. "Time's up, everybody. Mr. Everhart has a plane to catch."

Carl, too worn to make sense of Sharonda's gesture, nodded and turned his back on the crowd. And Sharonda. He walked toward the exit.

"Good work tonight." Carl stopped to shake the hand of one of the dancers.

"Mr. Everhart, we're done here." Alexis approached with his bags. Wasn't that why he paid this agent extra? She made decisions he sometimes didn't have the power to make in the height of the moment.

He was done: with New Hope, with his past, with—

"You would leave without saying goodbye?"

The disbelief in Sharonda's voice rose over the crowd and caused Carl to stop. He turned.

Sharonda took a step toward him. Her long hair, pulled over one shoulder, remained anchored with her white-and-gold hat. The swish of her hips made the off-white dress appear to dance. Gold heels completed the angelic look.

Alexis stepped in front of him. "I'm sorry, ladies. Mr. Everhart has—"

His angel took flight and left his agent sprawled on the ground.

⤙

Fight!

She ran out of her shoes, her focus on Carl Ray. Anything in her way became a casualty.

A woman cried out.

Sharonda crashed into his chest.

He grabbed her elbows to steady her.

"I'm not giving up," she said.

He raised a brow, gazed over her head, and cleared his throat.

Sharonda looked back at the path she'd taken. Her grandmother stood with her hand over her mouth, but Sharonda could still see she shook with laughter. Security guards gathered around the woman in the red jacket collapsed on the floor. A garment bag and a duffle kept her company, along with the hat that no longer occupied Sharonda's head.

She reached and grabbed air where the brim of her headpiece should have been. "Did I do that?"

"Yes." Carl wasn't laughing.

Lights flashed around the auditorium from all directions and voices rose in alarm.

Carl Ray grabbed her arm and pulled her through the exit.

She went head first into the back seat of a limo. He followed and slammed the door.

"Drive, plan B," he shouted. His arms wrapped around her seconds before the car jerked forward. "Are you okay?"

"What have I done?" The numb haze from the adrenaline rush lifted.

Carl Ray snatched Sharonda's purse hanging at her side and set it in her lap. "Call your mother and let her know you're with me. I need to contact Alexis when you finish." He released her to fasten his seatbelt.

Sharonda touched the side of her head. If only she could piece her thoughts together and make sense of what went wrong. Carl Ray had never handled her so rough.

She dug in her purse for her phone. She slid away from him. "Who's Alexis? And why not call her from your cell?"

"My duffel bag with my phone is still in the auditorium."

Sharonda's call went straight to voicemail. "Mom, I'm fine. I'm with Carl Ray headed …"

"I'll drop you off at your house." He kept his gaze forward.

"Home." Sharonda managed to say right before the recording ended. He stuck his hand out.

"What?"

"Your phone?"

This was not how she'd imagined things. What happened to happily ever after? She slapped the cell against his palm. Why was he so upset?

"Call me at this number when it's best to swing back through and pick you up." He laid the phone down between them. "What happened back there?"

"Where are we going?"

"On a route to shake any followers. Drop you off at home. I'll head back to the church to pick up my agent. Board a jet. And back to New York. Is that enough information for you?"

"I get it. I made a scene back there, but you don't have to be mean." His crass attitude cracked the last of her resolve. For the entire day, she'd functioned under a mindset to fight. And like a typical heavyweight, she'd played herself out. Sharonda slumped in her seat and stared out the window. *I'm on the ropes, Lord. If you don't fix things, they'll be forever broken.*

"Fine." She counted the stoplights until they merged onto Loop 49.

"Why were you coming for my autograph?"

"What?"

"I saw the pad. And why did you tackle my agent?" He gazed at her sideways.

"That *notepad* belonged to my grandmother and for your information, I didn't even see him."

"My new agent is a *her*. And you couldn't have missed the red jacket."

The lady in red on the floor. Sharonda cupped her cheek. "I wasn't thinking. What if she's hurt? People pulled out their phones." Her chest heaved.

"Shhhh." Carl Ray reached for her hand. "Breathe."

"I'm so sorry, but you were leaving. I couldn't bear to see you walk out of my life again. Please, Carl Ray, I was wrong, but everyone deserves a second chance."

"Sharonda, if you don't slow down, you're going to make yourself sick." He unclicked his seat belt and slid next to her. "Now take a deep breath."

He chuckled.

"What?"

He looked into her eyes. "When I turned and saw you standing there, you looked like an angel. Sharonda, you're so *beautiful*. And when you took flight …" He chuckled again, then turned somber. "What did you mean by, 'I'm not giving up?'"

She nestled closer, yet he remained aloof. "I was fighting. So, I ran. And I'm not going to stop, so hold me, Carl Ray. Fight for *us* like you asked me to." She caressed his cheek. "Tell me goodbye again. Like you did in my office the day you left."

He pulled away. "You're not making sense."

She took both of his hands into hers. "That wasn't a goodbye kiss. You were giving me an option, fight for us or leave. I didn't know how to fight then, but I'm learning. My technique isn't pretty. I run people over. But I'll get better with practice."

He smiled. "I wouldn't know what good technique looks like. No one has ever fought for me."

She leaned in slow and kissed his cheek. "If you'll have me, I will. I called Brice and broke the engagement. Mother knows I love you. All I'm asking is that you allow me to redo my goodbye, my answer." She lowered her gaze to their clasped hands.

He pulled her across his lap, nestled his face in the groove of her neck, and rocked.

She clung to him and waited.

Carl raised his head. "I've learned to live with abandonment, but I won't in a wife. I need more. When I come home off tour, I need you to be there. Or travel with me."

She softened her words. "I'm not your parents. Any of them. I am the woman who loves you. In this, you'll have to put your trust in Him. Can you do that?" She prayed silently.

He tightened his arms around her. "Goodbye, Sharonda Peterson." He feathered soft kisses over her lips. "Hello, Mrs. Carl Ray Everhart." He claimed them.

She deepened the kiss, sharing her surrendered heart with his.

"I'll have you," he whispered. "Not for one night but for a lifetime to show you just how much I love you."

9 781645 261841